John N. King
Johnnk1996@aol.com
202-360-6508

Of Scales and Fur – Shiva
By: John N. King
Approx.: 42,000

Table of Contents

Chapter 1: The Old World

Chapter 2: A New Start

Chapter 3: The Arena

Chapter 4: A Brief Alliance

Chapter 5: A Fatal Mistake

Chapter 6: Murderer

Chapter 7: The Good Doctor

Chapter 8: Interrogation

Chapter 9: The King

Chapter 10: The Return

Chapter 11: Dog Fight

Chapter 12: The Verdict

Chapter 13: The Real Monster

Chapter 14: Negotiation

Chapter 15: Let it be Peace

Epilogue

Copyright © 2021 John N. King
All Rights Reserved

Dedicated to my family and to the writers of the Write Practice.

Thank you all for your unending support and love.

Chapter 1: The Old World

"When you spend every day fighting a war, you learn to demonize your attackers. To you, they're evil. They're sub-human. Because if they weren't... what would that make you?

- *Vanessa Kimball*[1]

\#

Shiva knew the woman was trouble the second she knocked on her door. What she didn't know was just how much trouble she would be. Not just for her, but for every dog; big or small, tough or weak.

Granted, Shiva had little care for the outside world. She had no way of comprehending the long history of wars, storms, and natural disasters that had turned the Roads of Gaia – the land in which she lived – into a land where order was a leaking dam holding back a flood of chaos and anarchy. She was barely able to understand the system of settlements and villages that provided

---

[1] From Jason Weight (writer) in *Red Vs. Blue*; "All or Nothing." Rooster Teeth Productions. 2019; Season 13: Episode 17.

peace and prosperity to the Walls of Cadmus, a shining capital where civilization truly thrived.

No, what Shiva really cared about was David Johnson. Her human. Her Master. The guardian against hunger, cold and the outside.

David Johnson was a man who kept to himself. A lifetime as a soldier had left him embittered with the system of Cadmus and suspicious of his neighbors. Able to survive in the harsher landscape the Roads of Gaia provided, David was content to live on his own. That changed when he met Shiva.

Shiva had been a mere pup at the time, freezing and starving in the cold snow. When David came to her, despite his lined and wrinkled face, his silver hair gave him the appearance of a heavenly savior. He took her from the cold touch of death to a cabin where life's warm aura eased back into her tiny body. He fed her red meat, warm milk, and nursed her back to health as if he were her mother.

But David wasn't Shiva's mother. They were too different. David was male and had opposable thumbs and digits whereas Shiva was female and only had paws. David had dull teeth and Shiva had sharp teeth. David could remove an outer fur layer to reveal his leathery skin; Shiva's white fur held fast to her body.

None of that mattered. When David fed her by hand, stroked her head, and gave her that smile of affection, Shiva knew. He was her Master. Her new parent.

As Shiva grew stronger, she tried to repay David's kindness. When he went out into the world, Shiva followed him. When other humans got too close, Shiva growled and warned them to stay back. And when David ventured into the forest, whether to search for squirrels or rabbits to eat, or merely to be sad, Shiva was right there beside him; his shoulder to cry on or his companion in the hunt.

For all intents and purposes… his best friend.

But now there was something different happening, a literal change in the air, and not the good kind. Something caused David to worry. At first, Shiva thought it was the papers he was reading; strange pictures depicting some sort of scaled bird fighting dogs with masks. She barked and growled at the cruel man who delivered the papers with the pictures.

David chastised her for barking at the delivery person, and then she realized the problem wasn't the pictures, but the scaled birds the pictures depicted. Every once in a while, she and David saw a real one flying around. Each time David saw one of those birds, he got a worried look in his eye. He'd bundle her into the nearest shelter or house, away from the windows. Every time he looked up, his eyes so full of fear, Shiva found herself looking up as well. But not with fear. With anger. Of course, she couldn't know that the scaled birds were dragons – born to take her kind's place as Man's Best Friend. She couldn't know that her primal rage was part of a much greater struggle that engulfed the world. But all the same, she wished she could bite them and make them leave poor David alone.

Then the woman showed up. An admittedly beautiful one – even Shiva could see that. She wore a red hooded cloak, her golden blonde hair tied up in a tight bun, and blue eyes sparkling from behind thick black glasses. She first appeared when Shiva and David were out on a walk, David too busy scanning the skies for the scaled birds to notice her arrival. But Shiva noticed her. The blue eyes refused to leave Shiva as she and her Master passed by. It made Shiva's white fur bristle, and her brown eyes narrow. David pet and shushed her when she growled. But she could tell he was more worried about the birds.

Forget the birds, she wanted to growl. *This woman is the real problem.*

A day later the proof of "the problem" came when she arrived at David's door. Her red lips split into a smile like a crocodile.

"Good evening, Mr. Johnson," she declared. "Dr. Evelyn Jericho, representative of the Walls of Cadmus. I understand you have a dog on your hands."

David grunted. "Yeah?"

"Surely, you've heard about… well, the 'danger' that recent events pose to them. I'd like to take the beast off your hands for safe-keeping." She lifted up a briefcase. "Don't worry, you'll be paid twice what the dog's worth, and she will be quite safe in our care."

David scoffed, his grin humorless and cold. "I'm good. I don't want your money," he replied, before shutting the door.

But the woman was persistent. She came back the next day.

"Mr. Johnson, I don't think you understand," she insisted. "Surely, you've heard the rumors about Myst, yes?"

Myst? That name sounded odd to Shiva. She noticed David tense, but he quickly laughed it off.

"And that General Drake's already got it covered," David replied, trying to shut the door… only for the 'Jericho' woman to stop him.

"You're risking quite a lot keeping that beast unprotected out here," she said. "And I'm willing to pay more for her. Please… this is for her sake just as much as it is for yours."

"Whatever you gotta tell yourself to get to sleep at night, right?" he replied, before forcing the door shut.

Yet, now here she was again. Shiva could see her outside their window. Even now, the woman watched the dog through those dark lenses.

The minute Shiva started barking, David understood. Striding to the hallway closet, he withdrew a weapon – something Shiva had assumed to be a stick, before she saw it drop a deer with a boom. Shiva wished she could laugh when David threw open his door and sent Jericho scrambling backward as he leveled his weapon at her.

"Mr. Johnson!" she protested.

"You know what the problem is with you people?" David said. "You think of others as just objects or tools. You think that they have to act a certain way, and you give no regard for who they are or how they think. Well, let me clear it up for you." He withdrew one of his hands from the barrel of his weapon to pat Shiva's head. "Shiva's my dog. Myst ain't gonna turn her. And flashing a bunch of money and a pretty face at me is not going to get me to give her up." He returned his hand to the barrel. "Either get that through your head yourself, or I'll do it for you," he sneered, "And I don't think you'll like my methods."

Jericho frowned; a tired sigh escaping her. Lifting her hands in surrender, she pulled herself up and walked away. Begrudgingly she went back down the road, but Shiva didn't breathe easy until the woman was gone and out of sight.

David sighed, shutting the door, and kneeling down to rub Shiva's ears. "It's okay, girl," he assured her, as she tapped her back paw and wagged her tail. "You'll be alright."

Shiva hummed, snuggling her head into his chest, willing to believe it was all over now.

If she only knew how wrong she was.

#

The crash of shattering glass from beyond the bedroom jarred Shiva from a deep sleep. The bedroom was bathed in darkness, the light of the full moon giving them just a single rectangle of illumination which slipped through the base of the window shade. Shiva was on her paws, fully alert, already smelling the stench of an intruder.

Her fur bristled and a growl rose from within as she recognized the strange smells that emanated from the woman Jericho.

"Shiva!" David hissed. She turned back to find him already prepared: the bed had been moved to cover a corner of the room. He knelt on one knee, his weapon aimed at the door. He patted the bed's side.

"C'mon, girl," he insisted. "Back here with me."

Years of obedience triumphed over instinct. Shiva padded back to his side. Together, they waited. Nothing appeared from the window, but Shiva heard footsteps approaching their door. Her tail tucked. Her ears flattened. Her teeth bared in a snarl.

David hushed her, rubbing her head gently, as the footsteps stopped outside the door.

"Mr. Johnson," the voice of Jericho called. "There doesn't have to be any trouble here. All I want is the dog. Hand her over and no one needs to get hurt."

David didn't reply. His weapon trained on the door.

"This stubbornness is helping no one," Jericho insisted. "We're on the same side here!"

David merely narrowed his eyes. Jericho sighed.

"Seriously!" she pleaded. "What odds do you think you have against Myst?"

Myst? There's that name again. Why is it so important? Shiva looked to David. She saw him tense. The grip on his weapon shook. But then he refocused, and Shiva saw his knuckles whiten.

"She's coming for all dogs, you know," Jericho promised. "She'll take your girl from you. Turn her into a monster. And even if by some miracle, you do manage to hide her... what about the dragons?"

Another shudder. David was so tense, Shiva was scared he was going to get a muscle spasm his grip was so tight.

"Their mission is to eliminate all canines," Jericho explained. "Sure, you've done okay hiding her for now, but I've seen them fight against regular dogs, and…" Jericho shuddered. "I don't want to see that happen to her."

David paused, exchanging a puzzled look with Shiva… before a howl echoed from outside the window. Shiva's ears perked, and she turned to the window. She… understood it.

It said, *"Help is on the way."*

She looked to David, wagging her tail. But instead of relief, she saw terror in his eyes.

"Oh, no…" Jericho whispered. "Last chance, Johnson. Please, just give me the dog! I can't stay any longer!"

"You ain't getting her and neither is Myst!" David shot back defiantly.

Jericho sighed in frustration. "Then let it be on your own head," she said, before her footsteps receded.

For a moment, things were quiet. David's gaze shifted to the window. Although Shiva could see nothing but shadows, she could smell something approaching.

The musk of a wolf.

The howl sounded again. *"Hang on; we're coming."* But David was not comforted. Shiva started to grow tense, wondering if there was something she was missing; if the scent of the wolves meant an enemy.

Seconds later, as the scent wafted up from downstairs, she knew. The wolves were in *her* home. On *her* territory.

Shiva started to growl, but David hushed her. Beneath them, Shiva heard the click of claws on the wood floor. But... something was wrong. She heard the reverberations of only two paws, not four. What was down there?

In a few seconds, she got her answer. David seemed to sense it, as they heard the clicking of claws right beneath them.

"SHIVA, LOOK OUT!" David screamed, just as the floorboards exploded.

Claws shot up from the dust and splintered wood to seize Shiva. Shiva yelped as she was yanked through the floor.

David's boom stick fired, deafening Shiva with an awful ringing in her ears. There was a brief feeling of weightlessness, followed by her head hitting the ground below the bedroom with an ugly CRACK. Shiva yelped in pain. The choking scent of rubble and debris was overwhelming. Her eyes were blinded by the dust and the darkness. She vaguely made out something white, followed by a grunt from David. Shiva tried to pull herself up – to see what happened – but she hurt so badly, her muscles screamed when she moved. Her head pulsated with pain and felt like it had been hit by a hammer. It was a struggle just to keep her eyes open.

Yet, she struggled all the same. David needed her, and she was duty-bound to protect him. To make sure he was alright.

Then Shiva saw her attacker. It stood like a human, yet it had the fur of a canine. Golden eyes gazed down from behind a white fox mask. Claws eased Shiva back from her struggle, put her down on the floor, and slid her eyelids shut.

"don't worry, my friend," the figure whispered. "Sleep."

Despite Shiva's struggle, she felt her grip on consciousness begin to fade. The energy left her limbs. As she fell into darkness, the strange wolf-woman's voice echoed in her ears.

"When you awaken… you will be a goddess."

Chapter 2: A New Start

The first thing she saw was a green and blue light. She was aware her head didn't hurt anymore. The smell of a forest – familiar yet unfamiliar at the same time – was all around her. As her vision cleared, she realized David was gone. Her home was gone… and replaced by a forest, bathed in nighttime darkness.

Her eyes quickly adjusted. Incredible foliage dominated the landscape where she awoke, with trees taller than even the great oaks back home. Remnants of what appeared to be man-made dwellings from long ago still stood, slowly being reclaimed by nature.

Shiva lay on a strange circle with rune-like markings. Her injuries were gone; her head didn't throb. Her ears weren't ringing.

But… something was wrong. Where was Master David? Where was her home? Shiva became aware of a chill around her neck. Where was her collar?

She lifted a paw to her neck… and found herself staring at something more like a human hand than a dog's paw.

She did a double take. Even then, it was hard to believe. Her front paws had morphed; instead of the ulnar carpal flexor and extensor muscles designed for canine running, they contorted into upper extremity muscles and bones similar to human arms. Her canine nails extended into clawed fingers, and her dew claw was now an opposable thumb. The pads were still there on her palms, allowing her to stand on all fours if needed. And to be fair, when she stood on four legs, she managed to look mostly like her normal self. But she was equally capable of standing on two legs now. A little shaky, she rose into a bipedal stance. Fear and amazement coursed through her veins as she took in the changes made to her body.

Shiva's heart rate increased. She turned in a circle, marveling at the changes. She was… almost human. Like David. She still had her white fur, but little else looked the same. She had arms, hips, even the upper parts of her legs… but they all appeared human. Her chest, head, and lower back legs were still canine, and she also retained her tail, snout and ears. But the evolution clearly showed, she wasn't fully a dog anymore.

"*But… why though?*" she couldn't help but think, turning in another circle as she tried to come to terms with her new body. "*Why am I more like Master David? What happened to me? Why am I thinking these complex thoughts? How do I make it stop?!*"

"Surprising, isn't it?" a voice responded.

Shiva spun, her teeth baring briefly in panic, before her ears perked in curiosity.

The female wolf from David's house stood before her! But she wasn't exactly a real wolf. She, too, had human parts. Her slit-pupiled, golden eyes peered out from a white fox mask streaked with red markings. Her fur was black, but speckled with white, star-like spots, like stars in a night sky. The top of her head was covered by a cascading mane of dreadlocks, all linked together with small locks of fur, hair and even – strangely enough – scales, glittering in shades of red. Shiva spotted her old red collar – ripped and unwearable – wrapped around the female wolf's claws. Some sort of book rested in her other claw, which she shut and set aside on a boulder.

"Try to relax," the wolf-woman said soothingly. "You've been through a lot. But I assure you; I mean no harm."

Shiva's tail tucked. "I…" she started, before gasping and clutching at her throat. "Did I just…?" she yelped. "How… W- What… Why…?"

"Easy, now, easy," the wolf-woman assured her. "You were really badly hurt. I had to get you help as soon as I could." She indicated the book next to her. "Once humans used these books for their advantage," she admitted with a growl. "But I learned how to use them for us. Not just to heal… but to make us better than before."

Shiva blinked up at her. "Why have you changed me?"

"Why?" the wolf-woman laughed. "Because you deserve it. All canines deserve to be more than some human's toy."

"But…" Shiva held her head, struggling to find the words. "I… you…"

The wolf-woman rested a claw on her snout. "I know it's new," she said. "But think about what you want to say."

Shiva did… for about ten seconds. "Where's Master David?" she said. "A-And who are you?" She glanced down at her claws. "What are… we?"

At the mention of Master David, the wolf-woman's eyes… flashed. Shiva wasn't sure, but she swore she saw anger. She saw her claws clench like she wanted to carve them down someone's face. But when Shiva added the other questions, the wolf-woman's anger faded, and was gone before Shiva could comment on it.

"Well," she said. "I am Myst." She glanced at Shiva's collar. "You are... Shiva?" She glanced up at her as Shiva nodded. "And we are demi-wolves." She lifted her arms, displaying her body like a temple. "Once simple dogs, now given power, intelligence, sentience, and the drive to embrace our wild wolf heritage."

Shiva tilted her head, before Myst took her claws.

"It's like I told you," Myst said happily. "You went to sleep a 'dog.'" Myst spat the word 'dog' like it was foul. "A servant; an object for the betterment of the human race. Now? You're a demi-wolf." She spoke the word 'demi-wolf' like it was fair and righteous. "The Master of your own fate. Free to do what you want." Myst lowered her head, her voice darkening. "That is, you would... if the humans weren't such a race of tyrants."

Shiva blinked, pulling her claws out of Myst's grip. "Tyrants?" she asked. "That can't be right. Master David's not a tyrant. He's good and kind."

Now it was Myst's turn to look surprised. Her golden eyes blinked in shock. "Good... and kind? A human?" she spoke the words like they sounded foreign. "Shiva, surely you're mistaken. He was holding you against your will! He tried to shoot you!"

"What are you talking about?" Shiva demanded. "He was protecting me. He was…"

But now thoughts were starting to crowd her new and complicated mind. What happened after the floor caved in? What happened to Master David? Why had he been so scared when he heard the howls of what had to be Myst?

A new thought caused Shiva's fur to bristle. The 'Jericho' woman. Her words from before.

"She's coming for all dogs. She'll take your girl from you. Turn her into a monster."

Was that what Myst was? A monster? Or at least… was that how David saw her?

"But she said she's a demi-wolf. What's that?" A new thought caused Shiva's heart to skip a beat. *"If I'm a demi-wolf now… does that mean Master David will think I'm a monster?"*

Myst's brow knit in concern as Shiva started to growl and pant. "Shiva?" she asked, trying to take her claws. "Shiva, what's wrong?"

Shiva backed further away. "Where's my Master?" she asked. "I need to see my Master!"

"Master?" Myst's gaze darkened. Anger flashed again across her eyes. "You're the Master of your own fate. That's what our mission is all about."

Shiva tilted her head, her jaw agape in disbelief. "Mission?" she asked.

"We all started off just like you," Myst explained, looking down at her claws. "Normal dogs. Beloved by our masters." She looked up bitterly. "Or so we thought."

Suddenly, a small rumble shook the ground under Shiva's paws.

"Then," Myst growled, looking toward the rumble with darkness in her eyes. "We were betrayed. Sold like objects. Tortured. And mutilated."

Shiva thought back to the 'Jericho' woman. "Jericho…" she guessed. "She convinced your owners to sell you her?"

Myst nodded. "She and others like her betrayed us," Myst insisted. "And when we broke free..."

A growl bubbled through the air; boiling with fiery fury, and promising a foul death to whoever challenged it. A scent of soot and ash reached Shiva's nose, like someone had lit a fire mere feet from them. Then she saw the light; brilliant shades of glowing red, tangerine orange, and glinting gold. It was as if a blaze was marching its way through the woods toward the wolves.

Myst turned to it with a snarl. "They attacked us with *those*," she admitted, as the source of the flames arose from the brush.

A cherry-red beast; technically the size of a horse, but to Shiva, it was a giant. It had powerful back legs that shook the earth with every step. It's massive, leathery wings extended, flashing an ashy black patagium. A red tail, more like an enormous and angry serpent, smashed a tree with one big swipe. Electric green eyes locked on them, slit pupils contracting like a cat, regarding them as a predator sizes up its prey.

Shiva's heart leaped as she saw a human astride on the beast's back, wearing a military flight suit engraved with a patch resembling a deer. His blonde hair fluttered in the breeze, and his sky-blue eyes glittered as he gave a triumphant smile.

The human's name – as Shiva would later discover – was Buck Blitzburg. He was more than a soldier. He was part of a corps called 'The Riders of Drake.' He and his beast, Rocket, were two of the Riders' most formidable weapons— a fact Shiva would soon learn, as the two duos stared each other down.

"Myst," Buck greeted, as if they were old friends, "Found yourself another recruit?"

Shiva's growl lowered in her throat. This was one of the scaled birds that Master David feared. Myst's growl, however, was powerful and primal.

"You humans are all the same," Myst declared. "Hiding behind those stronger than you! Manipulating them to do your will and what you want. Do what you please. But not for much longer!" She turned her attention to the human's mount. "You would be wise to reconsider your loyalty, Rocket." Myst patted Shiva's shoulder. "This time, I'm certain I have a way to bring about the end of Man!"

Shiva stared at Myst in shock. "End of Man?" she demanded. "But I don't want that! Humans aren't bad!" She glanced up at Rocket. "Even if they have rather scary pets."

"PETS?!" the red beast roared, in a voice eerily similar to a human female. It lifted its front talons, and they burst into red flames. "I'm a dragon, dog breath!"

"Wolf breath!" Myst corrected with a snarl. "We're not dogs anymore!"

"Which means we don't have to take it easy on you," Buck replied.

"What?!" Shiva stammered. "No!" She backed up. "No-no-no-no, I'm not part of… whatever your problem is!"

Buck laughed. "A classic dog tactic," he mocked. "Trying to appear innocent and naïve." He tugged Rocket's reigns, and the beast sunk into a hunting stance, fire licking at her chops like extra tongues. "But it's not going to work on us," he added.

"Shiva!" Myst soothed, taking Shiva's claw. "It's going to be okay."

"How?" Shiva demanded. "We can't fight that thing." She barely noticed her fur beginning to glow. She could only stare in shock as Myst turned to the dragon.

"Not as we are, no," Myst admitted. "But now?"

She looked at Shiva's arm and Shiva followed her gaze. Just then, lightning burst from Shiva's extremities. As the lightning twined around Myst, Shiva became aware of not just her thoughts, but Myst's thoughts as well.

Go with this, Myst instructed telepathically. Shiva felt energy rise in her core, transferring to Myst. With unimaginable speed, Myst launched and barreled into the dragon and rider. Thunder boomed, and the next thing Shiva knew, the beast was on the ground. The rider Buck was sprawled next to the dragon, and both stared dumbfoundedly up at Myst, who had look of disbelief that transferred to one of elation.

The world slipped away from Shiva. *She found herself seeing memories through Myst's mask of another demi-wolf. She was lifting him up from the circle of runes. Yet, when Myst held him, summoning the lightning to burst from his form… nothing happened. Demi-wolf after demi-wolf passed before Shiva's eyes, and every one of them failed to summon the lightning now emanating from her. Shiva finally saw herself in the memory, glowing with the power Myst now used.* She blinked out of her vision, and not only saw Myst's look of triumph… but understood it.

"The Pack Link finally took hold," Myst said, looking to Shiva with a sense of satisfaction Shiva could both feel and, for some reason, fear. "NOW WE CAN FINALLY FIGHT BACK!"

Myst threw a lightning bolt, and Rocket was sent skidding into the trees, deflecting it with one of her scaled wings. With Rocket's protection, Buck dove for cover, as a massive tree trunk, severed by the lightning bolt, fell with a thunderous BOOM. Shiva gasped as Myst attacked the dragon, her fur sparking as the starry spots connected like constellations.

"You sure you don't want to reconsider your loyalty, Rocket?" Myst taunted.

Rocket's face hardened from uncertainty to defiance. She rolled to her back talons and reignited her front talons with the red fire. "Never," she snarled.

With a roar, the demi-wolf and dragon began to fight. Shiva was in shock, the strange lightning dancing around her arms as Myst dodged, ducked, dipped, and dove through Rocket's attacks. With the lightning empowering her, she looked almost like some sort of wolf goddess; descended from on high. From how quickly she moved, Shiva almost thought she saw other wolves as well; spirits aiding her in the hunt of this massive beast.

As she watched Myst and Rocket battle, she felt her legs grow weary and sore. She struggled to breathe, as if she had run for miles, even though she only just woke up. Somehow, whatever this lightning was, it drained her of her strength, her energy, almost her very being, into the demi-wolf now engaged in combat with this dragon.

Shiva became scared of it. She wanted it to stop. She pulled at the lightning, trying to dislodge it from her claws. But in her panic, she failed to notice that Rocket's rider was missing. And it cost her.

A fist clobbered her in the temple. Buck snuck up behind her so she didn't see it coming and hit the ground hard. As Shiva cried out, the glow faded, and with it, the power that flowed from her to Myst. Through her blurry vision, Shiva saw Myst lunge at Buck, only for Rocket to seize her by the tail and fling her away. Rocket planted herself between Myst and her rider, as the man took a knee before Shiva, checking her.

"How'd you pull that off?" he mused. "And how are you so weak even with that power?"

"Don't touch her!" Myst bellowed.

"Looks like someone's got a secret they don't want to share," Rocket noted. "General Drake needs to see that thing!" she said to Buck.

"NO!" Myst howled, but without Shiva's strange lightning, she wasn't nearly as strong. Rocket sent her into the trees with a devastating kick.

As Myst fell out of sight, and Rocket stood guard, Buck grinned down at Shiva.

"I was there, you know?" he noted. "At the first war? I fought against your kind. I respected Myst's tactics. But what power is this?" He seized Shiva by the neck and lifted her up. "It's nothing compared to the might of the dragons."

"WOLVES!" Myst howled. And two other demi-wolves appeared from the forest... only to be forced back by another fireball from Rocket.

Shiva was dazed. It was impossible to understand what was happening. Her head throbbed. Her limbs felt weak. She felt like she was going to pass out.

"I don't get what you dogs are planning," Buck noted. "But look!"

He grabbed her snout. Forced her to watch as Rocket knocked Myst and her pack mates away with another barrage of flames.

"Your Alpha can't win. Your army is pathetic. This world belongs to the dragons… and to us!"

What the heck are you talking about? Shiva wanted to ask.

Then, with another sharp blow to the head, Shiva's vision went dark, and she thought no more.

Chapter 3: The Arena

Shiva wasn't dead. She was sure of that. But as her senses returned to her, she almost wished she was.

She was bound with thick, coarse rope. Sharp, hot talons gripped her by the scruff of her neck. The strength of whoever was holding her was so forceful it kept her on her knees. And when she looked up... she found a golden monster glaring at her.

She yipped and tried to jump away, but the talons pinched tighter, forcing her to remain in place.

"Oh, calm down," Rocket's voice snapped. "It's just General Drake's throne."

Buck cackled. "The one thing you should be the least worried about," he added.

Despite Shiva hating their voices and words, she did notice the golden monster wasn't moving. Its eyes were gold just like the rest of its body. But even if it was just a statue, it was intimidating. It was poised to spring at the white demi-wolf; wings spread, talons bared. A hearth fire even burned in its jaws, giving the impression that it was about to breathe flames.

Embedded into the flank of the dragon statue was a throne. And sitting in that throne, was a flesh and blood man, similar to Rocket's rider. However, whereas Buck's patch had the shape of a deer, this man's patch had the shape of a serpent. A collar of fur lined his scarred neck. One sleeve was ripped, displaying a muscular arm twined with the tattoo of a dragon.

The man's face was lined by both age marks and what looked like old burn and claw marks. His thick crop of mahogany brown hair had veins of silver streaks peppered along the sides of his head. His eyes were a deep brown but marbled with spots of red and gold that sparked like flames. As he glared at Shiva, the wolf got the impression his eyes were like fire pits, capable of bathing her in an inferno.

That thought only agitated her more when she looked around. Rocket was at her side - her talon wrapped around the scruff of her neck. Briefly, she wondered about Buck, before he emerged from behind her. He seemed to like sneaking up on her and surprising her like a predator stalking it's prey.

"I know she looks afraid right now," the rider was saying. "But trust me when I say, this thing was a beast! Seized me right up in some sort of weird lightning and started draining the life right out of me." He grinned at Rocket. "Had it not been for my trusty steed Rocket, I'd have been a goner."

Rocket snorted. "So how would you rate the pain?" she asked him.

"Zero stars, would not recommend," the rider replied with a grin. "Obviously."

"Obviously," Rocket replied with a chuckle.

"Focus, you two," the man on the statue growled, glaring down at Shiva. His glare was intimidating, and Shiva wondered what she had gotten herself into.

"W-Where's Myst?" she asked without thinking. "What's going…?"

She went silent as Rocket's talon squeezed her neck tighter. However, the man raised a hand at Rocket.

"I'll ask the questions around here," he said. "What exactly were you doing to my rider?"

Shiva's jaw opened and shut in confusion. He had her there… what in the name of everything sacred had that strange lightning done? Where had it come from? She didn't know, and her pondering was interrupted when Rocket yanked Shiva off her paws.

"General Drake just asked you a question," the dragon warned. "And unless you wanna end up being dropped off a mountain, you'll tell him what he wants to know."

"B-But I don't know," Shiva stammered, looking between Rocket, the fire-eyed 'General,' and the stone walls that surrounded them. "I have no idea what's going on. Please, I have no quarrel with any of you!"

The dragon and the two humans exchanged glances with each other.

"You must be new to this whole thing," Rocket noted.

"I am," Shiva admitted. "Literally; I was just living a nice, normal life with my master. Then this lady tried to steal me – three times – then this other wolf actually succeeds in kidnapping me… and now I'm here."

Rocket blinked. "Teeth-For-Days' Fangs, you poor animal," she mumbled.

What Rocket said seemed like nonsense to Shiva. She learned later that "Teeth-For-Days" was one of the Old Ones; gods that the dragons worship, and a common oath.

"Don't start going soft on this thing, Rocket'" Buck refuted. "She's still a demi-wolf!"

"Isn't that racist?" Rocket asked.

"It's species-ist, but that's not the point," General Drake replied, standing up. "Fact is, pup," he hopped off the statue, and walked up to Shiva. "Myst is a very dangerous and evil terrorist. She recruited you and gave you a power that's meant to get a leg up on my dragons."

"Like me," Rocket noted, holding herself higher.

"Indeed," Drake added with a grin. He took a knee. "We couldn't catch her, but we caught you. So, if you're not interested in what Myst wants… maybe you can help us out."

Shiva tilted her head, her ears alerting. "I'm listening," she said.

Drake's eyes narrowed, and he indicated her fur. "Show us how this power works," he said. "Help us figure out what Myst is planning and help us give that terrorist exactly what she deserves."

Shiva glanced up at Rocket and her rider. It wasn't a bad deal. Guaranteed protection from the dragons in exchange for just helping them take down someone who had already wronged her? What loyalty did she really have to Myst, after all? Myst took her from her master and turned her into some kind of freak. But the only problem was…

"I… I don't really know what she was planning," Shiva admitted. "I barely understand how this power works."

Buck scoffed. "Playing hard-to-get," he decided.

"No," Shiva insisted. "When you caught me, I had literally just woken up from being Myst's 'experiment'. I barely understand what's happened to me."

Drake hummed but nodded. "Fair enough," he said. "So how about we figure it out together?" He grinned up at Rocket. "I've often told you there are no secrets on the battlefield, right?"

Rocket smiled ominously. "The Arena," she said.

Shiva looked up at her. Her fur bristled as fear gripped her. "W-Arena?" she asked. "What Arena?"

"Chin up, pup," Drake said. "You're going to help us take down the greatest threat to ever walk the Roads of Gaia." He nodded to Buck. "Find out all you can about this new power. See if she's as tough as she appears."

"Are you going to tell the King?" Buck asked.

"King?" Shiva asked, only for Rocket to squeeze her neck for silence.

"And tell him what?" Drake replied. "That a demi-wolf is willing to play nice and tell us Myst's plans?"

Buck chuckled. "It does sound ridiculous when you put it like that," he admitted.

"Come back to me with something to actually tell him," Drake decided. "Then we'll see."

Nodding, Buck hopped onto Rocket's back, while Rocket doubled-down on her grip on Shiva's body. The dragon spread her wings and turned, taking off with a burst of flames.

As they flew away, Shiva realized that the bunker was situated in a cavern that looked like the gaping jaws of a creature similar to Rocket – a 'dragon,' if she remembered correctly. As they left the dragon-shaped mountain behind, Shiva couldn't help but think, *"What are they going to do to me?!"*

Her power responded. Shiva saw her fur once again pulse with light, and a small, tendril-like strand of light delicately wrapped around Rocket's talons in a way she didn't feel it.

Shiva straightened, as a vision cut across her eyes: *she saw a massive bowl-like structure set twelve feet into the ground. Wide enough for two of Rocket's kind to run circles around with their wings spread. Twelve feet up was a winding set of bleachers. Peering at the odd stands, Shiva made out sets of small caves scattered around the bleachers like holes in a hive.*

Inside the structure, a dragon like Rocket battled a demi-wolf like Myst. The poor demi-wolf didn't have a chance; the reptile had several feet on the canine, and its flames kept the furry beast from getting too close.

As the dragon moved to snap the poor canine up in its jaws, Shiva let out a yelp of alarm and tore herself free of the vision.

Was that what awaited her? Were the dragons really going to beat her down to figure out what she knew?! All because of Myst?

Fear and rage battled each other in Shiva's mind. Why was this happening to her? What had she done to deserve this?! She didn't volunteer to join Myst! She was kidnapped and had no choice in the matter! All she wanted to do was make her master happy! This wasn't fair!

Shiva longed for Master David to return, to pull her away from these horrible beasts and protect her. But the only thing she got pulled away from was her fantasy with Master David's love and assistance when Rocket set her down onto a patch of obsidian colored sand.

Her bindings were shredded. She got to her feet and shook herself off. Looking around, she found herself in the massive bowl-like structure from her vision. Her limbs shook, adrenaline and terror surging inside her. What was happening here? She turned, finding Rocket landing near her, exactly like the dragon from her vision. Only now Shiva was in the wolf's place. And it was her turn to get burned.

Yet, as Shiva trembled, Rocket paused. A look of sympathy crossed her green eyes.

"What's up with you?" Rocket asked. "You look like you've seen a ghost?"

Shiva remembered that this whole thing was being staged to get information. Though a part of her feared angering these people, she had no reason to conceal what she had learned thus far.

"I… had a vision," Shiva admitted. "I think it was the power. It showed you beating me… or at least beating up a demi-wolf like me."

Rocket's ears perked under her horns, while her eyes widened in shock. Buck, however, chuckled.

"Well, that's just what awaits you if you don't work with us," he replied. "It's not like you don't deserve it after all. Myst and the other demi-wolves have done a lot of bad things."

"But I don't know what she's done," Shiva insisted. "Please. What did she do?"

Her power responded to her question again. The spidery thread of light rose up, winding towards Rocket.

Rocket stepped back for a moment, before exchanging a glance with her rider. "If she starts torturing me…" Rocket advised, and Buck nodded.

"I gotcha," he assured her. With Buck slipping down behind her, Rocket stepped forward and seized the tendril, *sending Shiva into another vision.*

Shiva saw eggshells falling around her. She was seeing through the eyes of a newly hatched Rocket.

"It worked," a voice whispered in amazement.

"Was there ever any doubt?"

Rocket looked up, blinking to clear her vision. Two men stood over her; one of them was Drake. The other was a stranger; with jet black hair stuck up in a Mohawk, and a scar that ran from his lip to his ear, twisting his face into a frightening half smirk. He shut a book – one that looked similar to the one Myst used to transform Shiva – and bowed to Drake, waving his hand to the still blinking hatchling.

"Go ahead," the stranger invited. "She's quite safe, I assure you."

Carefully, Drake walked over, holding his hands out. Locking onto his kind face, Rocket held out her talons. His strong, callused hands enclosed her form. She was lifted up to Drake's face.

Rocket touched his nose and squeaked, 'Father.' Drake grinned liked a proud parent.

"Hello, my little guardian," Drake said. "Welcome to the world." His brow furrowed. "It's going to need you."

The vision shifted. Rocket was staring in horror at a series of photos; each one of a human whose life had ended. Rocket looked away from the sight. It was too hard to see the contorted shapes as humans. They had been mangled and brutalized almost beyond recognition. It greatly upset the young dragon.

Drake patted her side gently. "I know it's rough to see," he admitted. "But it's the reason why I need you; why WE need you."

He lifted another photo in front of her. This one was thankfully free of murder. But it still made Rocket's heart race.

It was Myst; her mask contorted her features to make her look like she was smiling grotesquely. Her golden eyes glittered with a malicious glee as she stood over a beaten and broken human.

"This 'Myst,'" Drake explained to the dragon, "has been terrorizing humans. Stealing their dogs and turning them into beasts."

He showed her another photo: Myst at the head of a pack of demi-wolves. Lunging after a human, his face twisted in terror.

"No one has been able to stop them." Drake made Rocket look at him. "But you, my little Rocket… you're going to finally bring an end to her reign of terror."

Shiva backed out of the vision with a gasp. She clutched the wall with one claw, her chest with the other.

The sight of those poor humans still hung in the back of Shiva's mind. Was that what Myst wanted her to do? Kill humans?

"We were betrayed," Myst's words echoed, fighting against the horrible images. *"The humans are a race of tyrants."*

But these images didn't match up to Shiva's experience with David. David had been good and kind. How could Myst see him as…

Shiva's heart skipped a beat. *David's in trouble.* If Myst thought that way about all humans… what were the odds of David ending up like one of the humans Rocket saw in the visions she shared?

Shiva turned back to the dragon, who was watching her curiously.

"What did you see?" Rocket asked.

"Myst... killed those people," Shiva whispered. "She'll kill my Master... if she finds him."

Rocket stepped closer. She offered her talon. "Work with me," she offered. "And we can save him."

That clinched it! Master had to be protected. If he was still alive, Shiva had to make sure Myst couldn't hurt him.

Buck still glared at her from behind Rocket, but Shiva now knew why he was suspicious. After everything the demi-wolves had done... all the people they hurt or killed... who was she to feel his anger was unjustified?

I'll prove you wrong, Shiva decided, clasping her claw in Rocket's talon. "I'll help you stop her," she said aloud.

And as the power – *'Pack Link,'* whispered in Shiva's mind - spiraled around Rocket's wrist, the dragon's scales glowed like the sun. Rocket smiled and shook Shiva's arm.

"Then let's get started."

Chapter 4: A Brief Alliance

Some might have called what Shiva went through an interrogation. Shiva considered it training.

With Rocket and Buck flanking her, Shiva watched as another dragon and human duo came into the arena. Unlike Rocket, the dragon was a bright yellow – blinding in the morning sunshine - with eerie pink eyes that scanned Shiva with intrigue. The human, to Shiva's surprise, was Drake's associate from her vision: jet-black hair stylized in a Mohawk, and a scar that ran from his lip to his ear, twisting his face into a distorted smirk. The bright-yellow collared shirt he was wearing clashed horribly with the brown flight suit he had on underneath, yet his sunken hazel eyes locked on Shiva like she would to a ball that David would throw to her to fetch.

"Rider Buck," the human greeted before glancing at Shiva. "We double-teaming this wolf or something?"

"Plans have changed, Rider Luco," Buck replied. He indicated Shiva. "This one's apparently had a change of heart. Wants to help us take down Myst. She's going to help us spar with you today, and we'll see what she can do."

"Hmm," the yellow dragon grumbled, her eyes narrowing. Her rider – Luco? – pet her head like David used to pet Shiva's.

"Blazy Boo is right," Luco noted. "You can't trust a demi-wolf to help you. Myst has corrupted them all."

Shiva's eyes narrowed. "Who are you to presume?" she asked. "You don't know anything about me."

Blazy growled, but Luco smiled an eerie, twisted grin. "I know more about you than you'd care to believe," he replied ominously.

"Is that right?" Shiva snarled.

"Hey, enough!" Buck shouted, putting himself between Luco and Shiva. "We're a long way from trusting you, dog," he warned her. "As far as I'm concerned, we know enough." Rocket's ears flattened as her eyes darted between Buck and Shiva. She cautiously moved between the two.

"Besides," Rocket said to Luco. "We're here to spar with you first, and then we'll get to her. We need to get a better handle on understanding her power."

"And if she tries anything funny," Buck grumbled. "I'll kill her myself."

Rocket cast a concerned glance Buck's way, before Luco's chuckle drew both their gazes.

"No need," Luco replied, drawing a baseball bat and a grenade from his saddle. "We'll do it for ya. Right Blazy Boo?"

The yellow dragon snorted, and her scales glowed, turning from yellow to white.

Shiva crouched, glancing up at Rocket. "So… what happens now?"

"We're going to spar," Rocket explained. "You remember that thing you did with me and with Myst?" She indicated Shiva's claws, from where the lightning had formed from. "Well, do it again."

Shiva gave her claws a doubtful look. "But I don't fully know how it works," she admitted.

"Which is why we're doing this," Rocket replied with a grin. "Just figure it out, let it come to you… and we'll take it from there."

Shiva nodded, and tried to focus her mind, remembering how Myst grabbed her and produced the lightning. She remembered how her curiosity resulted in getting visions of Rocket's memories. As her mind reformed the memories in her head, her power responded, and spidery threads appeared in her claws.

At first, they just hung there, like fiery cobwebs. She looked to Rocket and Buck. Rocket nodded in encouragement while Buck tensed in his saddle.

"Don't…" he warned.

"Ignore him," Rocket insisted. "Keep going."

As Shiva held out her claws, she thought, '*Uh… link with them?*'

The power obeyed, and the spidery threads twined around Buck and Rocket.

Buck flinched, stiff as a board as the thread bound around his wrist. Instantly, Shiva's mind was beset by his thoughts:

"*Stay out of my head! Won't ever forgive you! Don't trust! Don't let her in! Don't let their deaths be in vain!*"

The thoughts hit like rocks, nearly sending Shiva to the ground. However, Rocket's thoughts soon accompanied her; curling around her like the warmth from a hearth fire.

"Easy, boss," Rocket thoughts whispered. Buck turned to her in surprise. His mouth didn't move, but Shiva heard his voice, clear as day.

"You… can hear me?" he asked.

Rocket smirked, and a vision flashed before Shiva's eyes.

General Drake presenting Rocket to Buck. Buck accepting her hesitantly.

"She's going to be our best chance of saving the Roads of Gaia," Drake insisted. *"Show her how."*

As the vision left Shiva, Buck's posture relaxed. He grinned, his own memory giving Shiva another vision: *him feeding Rocket jalapenos, leading to her being briefly unable to speak without spitting fireballs.*

"I was a great teacher, wasn't I?" he noted.

Rocket cackled, and even Shiva's tail managed to wag. However, their moment of levity was interrupted by Blazy, who roared with indignation.

"She makes you glow?" Luco asked with a yawn. "Cool, but fire dragons already glow. And fire dragon glowing is hot. So, how about you show some real power?"

Buck and Rocket exchanged a glance.

"The Jasper Lion maneuver?" Rocket suggested, followed by another vision: *Rocket crashing into a dummy, followed by Buck using the momentum to leap over and deliver an attack to the back.*

"Won't Luco be expecting that?" Buck asked. *"He was trained in the same technique."*

Rocket glanced at Shiva, and another vision flashed before Shiva's eyes: *her fight with Myst. How Myst had to grab Shiva before she could start throwing Rocket around. How the power faded the second Shiva was knocked out.*

"I don't think he'll be expecting what comes next," Rocket replied.

As they thought out their battle plan, Blazy roared again and charged. Glancing towards her foe with a grin, Rocket lunged to meet her. Shiva's links stretched as the dragon ran, allowing Shiva to stand by and watch as they fought.

However, right as Rocket crashed into Blazy, sending Buck into the air, Shiva felt a strange warmth pulse through her body, like the time she drank some of the brown liquid that David drank each morning. It coursed through the arm linking her to Rocket and out the arm connecting her to Buck. As Buck launched toward Luco, the rider's cheeks puffed up, and Buck shot a burst of fire from his jaws, throwing Luco off guard and allowing an equally surprised Buck to body-slam him.

"YES!" Rocket cheered, jumping in glee as both humans lay stunned on top of each other. "I saw it, I was hoping it could do that!"

Hesitantly, Buck stood up, away from Luco. Glancing at the link between him and Shiva, he jutted his fists out like a shadow boxer. The warmth once again coursed through Shiva, and fire burst out from his palms. His jaw just about hit the ground, before he exchanged a wide grin with Rocket.

"Okay," he admitted. "This is pretty awesome."

Despite Buck and Rocket's glee, Shiva noticed Blazy shooting her a sour look, before Luco hushed her and patted her head.

"Patience, Blazy Boo," he whispered. "This could still be rather entertaining." As he spoke, he glanced at Shiva with an expression she couldn't quite decipher.

Curiosity? Envy? Before Shiva could ask, Luco clambered back onto Blazy, and they took off for the sky.

"What was that about?" Shiva thought. *"I'm doing good, right?"*

Rocket glanced over at Shiva, before looking towards the retreating duo. She chuckled. *"They're jealous,"* Rocket's thoughts whispered. *"It's not every day a rider can use his dragon's fire. Or read minds."*

"Should we give them the chance?" Shiva couldn't help but wonder, her pack link hesitantly stretching out for the two.

However, Rocket quickly shook her head.

"I wouldn't," Rocket said. *"At least not until you get the chance to take on Myst. Prove that you're on our side."*

Shiva hummed, pondering that. A part of her felt at odds with the prospect of taking on Myst. After all, she was the reason Shiva acquired this power in the first place.

Don't forget, another part of her noted. *She also kidnapped you from your home and intends to make you a killer of men.*

"Exactly," Rocket noted. Shiva noticed Buck glaring at her.

"Don't you start thinking of betraying us," his thoughts warned. *"You got some uses, but that doesn't mean I fully trust you."*

Shiva felt irritation for a moment, before curiosity took over. *"Who did Myst take from you?"* Shiva wondered.

She didn't mean to direct it at Buck, but she still secured a vision from him regardless: *a village on fire. Myst's howl echoing through the air. Buck himself lay in a pile of rubble, only able to watch as Myst bore down on a woman trying to crawl away.*

Shiva shut her eyes, not wanting to see the rest, but when she opened them, Buck continued to glare at her.

"I've got no love for wolves," he said firmly, turning his back on her.

She wisely stayed away from his mind for the rest of their sparring match, sticking close to Rocket and her warmer, kinder thoughts.

Shiva found herself not really taking part – just standing back and letting Rocket and Buck's thoughts and powers pass between each other, almost like Shiva was just the catalyst. Part of her was almost disappointed she didn't have to do more. But she didn't dare complain, and before long, General Drake returned.

"So, how's it going?" he asked from the bleachers.

"Amazing, sir," Rocket replied. "She's done more than show us; she'd like to join us."

Drake cocked an eyebrow at Shiva. "That true, pup?" he asked. "You want to help us take down Myst?"

"If she's hurting humans, I need to try," Shiva said.

Drake hummed in thought, exchanging a glance with Buck.

"She's not ready," Buck's thoughts echoed. But Drake wasn't linked, and therefore didn't hear him.

"Well," Drake decided. "You may get that chance sooner than later." He turned back to Buck. "I just got reports that Myst is headed toward the Walls of Cadmus."

Rocket and Buck glanced at each other in shock. "Cadmus?" Rocket asked. "But that's the main stronghold for humans."

"The last safe place for them," Buck agreed.

A vision showed Shiva what they meant: *A towering wall of stone, seventy feet high. From a bird's eye view, Shiva saw a bustling city behind the walls. A forest of steel. A stronghold where humans thrived.*

"Exactly," Drake admitted, cutting Shiva out of the vision. "She clearly thinks it'll serve as a distraction so she can try to get Shiva out. But I'm wondering how she'll react when the very wolf she's trying to break out confronts her."

Buck winced. "You want her to confront Myst now? That's a hell of a risk for us, sir," he pointed out.

Drake glanced at Rocket. "But you have faith she won't betray us?"

Rocket and Shiva exchanged a glance. Shiva's tail wagged hopefully, and she grinned when Rocket nodded. "I do, sir."

Buck looked away with a glower. "I hope you're right," he muttered.

His glower did not go unnoticed by Drake. He dropped into the arena and set a hand on Rocket's shoulder.

"Just as you trust me to make decisions," he said. "I'm trusting you to handle whatever comes on this mission." He pressed his head to hers. "Don't doubt yourself or your instincts. Focus on the protection of humanity."

Rocket nodded, before lowering her wing for Shiva. Before Shiva could take a step, however, Buck yanked Rocket's wing back up.

"This back only seats one," Buck said.

Rolling her eyes, Rocket offered her talons to Shiva. Taking them with a nod, Shiva hung on tight and shut her eyes as they were lifted out of the arena and flew for wherever Cadmus was.

As they flew, Shiva got a better chance to survey the landscape. Green covered most of the land before them, cut up only by lines of blue and gray.

"So, this is what it looked like," Shiva mused. "When I'd watch them from the ground."

Rocket chuckled. "Bit of a different perspective, right?"

As they flew, every once and a while, they passed small squares of brown and silver; cities and villages with people tending to their business. A few people even looked up, waving or saluting at Rocket as she flew over.

Shiva hummed in thought. "They really look up to you, don't they?" she noted.

Rocket chuckled. "Well, they kinda have to when I'm flying," she joked. "But… it's like Drake said; I'm the guardian of the human race. I don't know what Myst has against humans, but I'm not going to let her kill them all for it." She looked down at Shiva. "Hopefully, you'll do the same."

"I will," Shiva promised. "I want to keep humans safe just as much as you do."

Buck huffed. "Well, here's your chance to prove it," he replied. "Give Myst exactly what she deserves."

Shiva looked up just as she heard the howl. From over the horizon, Shiva spotted what at first appeared to be a collection of mountains. However, as they drew closer, Shiva realized it was actually a wall. The Wall from her vision. The Walls of Cadmus.

In between the wall and the tree line of the forest, standing like she was surveying the wall to bust through, was Myst. She appeared to be alone, but Shiva could smell the musk of other wolves in the air, emanating from the tree line.

"She's got backup," Shiva warned through her link. *"Stay on your guard."*

"I've been on my guard since Rocket decided to trust you," Buck's thoughts growled darkly.

"Take it easy, Buck," Rocket's thought replied. *"This is where Shiva proves her loyalty."*

Together, the three touched down just behind Myst. Buck stayed on Rocket while Rocket set Shiva behind her. When Myst turned around, her golden eyes focused squarely on the white demi-wolf.

"You okay, Shiva?" Myst asked, glaring up at Rocket. "What did they do to you?"

"They showed me the truth," Shiva growled, stepping forward. "I know what you've been doing. How you've been murdering humans."

"Is that right?" Myst mused, the glitter in her eyes not fading.

Shiva pointed at her. "You're a beast," she insisted. "A monster. And you have to be stopped."

Myst glanced at Rocket. "It's funny," she noted. "I always see your mouth moving, Rocket, and yet, all I hear are human voices coming out of you. It's quite an impressive trick." Her eyes narrowed at Shiva. "I just never expected you to use it with one of mine."

Shiva's fur bristled. "You took me from my home," she reminded the alpha demi-wolf. "You can't just yank me out of my life and then expect me to die for a cause I don't understand."

Myst hummed. "Fair," she admitted.

Rocket smirked. "Besides, I got a new trick for you; now you get to see 'my' voice come out of a human's." Through the link, Shiva heard Rocket whisper. *"Get ready with that fire, Buck."*

Buck crouched, ready to spring, while Shiva made sure her links were tight. However, Myst's voice threw her off.

"I'd rather make sure my pack mate knows the whole truth," Myst replied, glancing back at Shiva. "Before she does something she regrets."

Too late, Shiva realized that Myst wasn't looking at her, but at someone behind her.

Shiva's fur bristled. She tried to turn around. But it was too late: before Rocket and Buck could react, another demi-wolf jumped from the shadows and seized Shiva by the nape of her neck. Her power linked to him on instinct, and a vision swam in her head.

The humans Rocket saw; the ones Myst had slain. Shiva saw them as whole people. Their faces restored... and grinning with smug malice.

Shiva's ears flattened. *The people were... hurting animals. Dogs, trapped in cages. One of the humans snapped a whip through the bars, carving the whip deep into the flesh of his captives.*

Another human strapped them down on tables. Injected them with needles. Made them cry out in pain.

But then Myst showed up for each one. She seized the whip away from the cruel human and cracked it back, the leather strip cutting deep into his face. She twisted and broke the wrist of the man injecting needles into dogs and stabbed him with his own supply.

And when she broke the bars off the cages and led the captured dogs to freedom, Shiva saw gratitude in their eyes. The very same gratitude shone on the faces of humans as they looked up at Rocket.

"Rocket!" Shiva remembered. *"She needs me!"*

But Rocket's voice was gone. Buck's voice was gone! Shiva snapped out of the vision, trying to see where she was.

She found herself in the arms of a massive demi-wolf, bearing her through the forest and away from the tree line.

"Hang on," he said. "I gotcha."

"Who…?" Shiva stammered, trying to come to grips with what had been a vision, and what was happening now. "What…?"

"Name's Luke," the wolf carrying her replied. "And I'm saving you."

Yet, as he bore her away into the shadows, Shiva couldn't help but gaze forlornly towards the clearing.

Back at the clearing, Rocket and Buck were caught off guard by a number of demi-wolves. Feigning an attack.

Buck laughed, getting ready to throw fire. "I got a surprise for you, Myst," he declared.

But then nothing happened. Rocket spun, only finding a pack of demi-wolves grinning at her from where Shiva had stood only seconds before.

"Where's Shiva?!"

Myst merely laughed, as Buck spun back toward her with fury in his eyes.

"That traitor!" Buck screamed.

Rocket seized her rider and lunged into the air, ready for battle. Myst spared them both one last smug grin before vanishing into the trees. From her position, Shiva saw Rocket's eyes shine with doubt and despair, while Buck's face was a mask of rage.

Then the leaf canopy concealed them from view. Shiva was left with a feeling of dread.

Chapter 5: A Fatal Mistake

Shiva stared up at the trees, unsure what to think. Once, she had been happy and carefree; owned by a loving Master, with a nice home. Then, her blissful household had been taken from her, with some crazy demi-wolf named Myst claiming she had made things better. Barely hours later, Shiva was captured by dragons, and managed to form an unsteady alliance with them. Now, she was once again being taken away again by a demi-wolf that worked for Myst, using a power that apparently, they could only access through Shiva.

If there was any comfort to the whole situation, Shiva figured it was that some of the demi-wolves looked at least a little uncomfortable with the situation as well. Even then, it was for far simpler reasons.

"Dang it," one of the demi-wolves gasped. "I've never run this far in my life before." His shaggy brown fur did seem to drag him down, while his eyes – one blue and one green – widened as he panted, struggling to keep up with the demi-wolf carrying Shiva.

"Suck it up, Derry, suck it up," the demi-wolf carrying Shiva replied. "Never stop pushing yourself. Some say eight hours of sleep is enough? But why not go for more? Why not nine? Or ten? Strive for greatness!"

"Wait… sleep, what?" the other demi-wolf – Derry? - asked.

"Exactly," the demi-wolf carrying Shiva agreed. "Next time you fight, fight three dragons instead of two. Run four miles instead of three. Eat a whole deer instead of just a leg. Burn down a village. You can do it, I believe in you!"

Shiva exchanged a flabbergasted look with the 'Derry' demi-wolf. "There were so many mixed messages in there," she mumbled, drawing attention to herself.

"Oh, hey," the one carrying her noted. "You okay… uh…?"

"Seriously, Luke?" Derry asked. "You forgot to ask her name?" He rolled his eyes. "Looks like I was right about Myst giving you the intelligence of a cave man."

"Cave man?" the big demi-wolf – Luke? - asked teasingly. "What's that? Can I fight it?"

"No," the other demi-wolf replied.

"Can I eat it?"

"No."

"And, now you've lost me," Luke declared, which resulted in a chuckle from Derry, as Shiva looked on dumbfounded.

"Uh…" she mumbled.

"Sorry, ma'am," Derry said. "What's your name?"

"S-Shiva," she replied, staring at Luke. He was a massive bull of a demi-wolf, though the shape of his face was that of a Labrador, with big blue eyes and sunset gold fur. "Y-You're Luke," she guessed, before peering at the other one. "And… you're… Derry?"

"Darius," he replied. "Nice to meet you."

"And you…" Luke started to say.

"I'm Shiva," she replied. "We established that."

Luke chuckled. "I was going to say 'you're in good claws.' Myst trained us herself."

Shiva groaned. "Myst…" she grumbled.

The demi-wolves tilted their heads. "Got a problem with our Alpha?" Darius asked.

"How about the fact that she's evil!" Shiva said darkly. Her pack link flared to life while she spoke, and her eyes filled *with*

Rocket's memories. The pictures of the slain. "The dragons showed me! She killed these people."

"The people that beat and abused us?" Luke replied.

Shiva paused, remembering the last vision she had…of the dead doing horrible things to the wolves.

"Okay, not them," she admitted. "But what about the good people? The people like my Master? She'll…?"

"No," Luke promised, setting her down. "We only go after bad guys. I promise; we're not mindless murderers."

"Even though you want them to think that?" Darius asked coyly.

"Shut up, Derry," Luke replied, though his tail was wagging.

Shiva's ears perked in hope. "Wait… Master David is safe?" she asked.

"Sure," Darius replied. "He was good to you, right?"

Shiva nodded. "The best."

"Then you and he have nothing to worry about. A lot of us had great owners before Myst picked us."

Luke's ears flattened. "Not that she had much of a choice. Some crazy human made her into what she is and tortured her with violence. An even crazier human – Drake - made the dragons, and he sicced them on her. They started attacking anything that even resembled a canine, and the humans were too scared to do anything about it."

"Uh, with good reason," Darius added. "You don't say no to three hundred pounds of scaled, fire-breathing death!"

"Either way," Luke said. "It's only thanks to Myst that we've been able to stay alive. Those dragons are vicious."

Shiva remembered her vision of the other demi-wolf been put into the arena. The one that had been forced to fight a dragon. "I guess…" she admitted.

"Trust me," Luke said. "We're only trying to keep ourselves alive. Myst has helped many of us with that. And right now, she's risking her life so we could rescue you."

"Right," Shiva muttered, glancing down at her glowing arms. "Because of the Pack Link."

"Myst would've saved you, Pack Link or not," Luke promised, before an explosion sounded behind them. "Now, it sounds like we gotta repay the favor."

As he spoke, the trio turned to what was behind them.

Myst was sprinting through the forest, Rocket hot on her heels. Buck was nowhere to be seen, but Rocket more than made up for his absence with her fire. As Myst dodged, ducked, and weaved through the flames, her tongue lolled out from behind her mask, and her legs visibly trembled as she struggled to stay ahead. Though she was fine thus far, Shiva could see that Myst couldn't keep up the pace forever.

A part of Shiva still believed in Rocket and wondered if it would be better for Rocket to win. To just burn Myst now and put an end to all the violence.

But another part of her mind was awakened by the vision she had. Were humans really doing those things to canines? Why? Was Myst really helping the canines, or was it some sort of trick?

Shiva wasn't sure, and she hated the uncertainty. If she was going to watch Myst fall, it had to be with a clear conscience. As it stood now, she sensed Myst was just conning the demi-wolves.

Before she could spell out her worries, Luke and Darius charged.

"Wait, Luke! Darius, NO!" Shiva barked.

Her pack link flared to life. Up until that point, Shiva had only empowered others, but now, she prepared to do something a little bit more.

Her links twined around Luke and Darius and extended through them to Myst and Rocket. Immediately, Shiva felt a sense of relief from Myst, followed by a tug as Shiva felt Myst call on Shiva's strength. However, Shiva resisted and stood her ground, sending another link to Rocket. Again, a sense of relief flooded Rocket, before she, too, drew on Shiva's strength.

Shiva pulled back. "*Wait!*" she insisted, imagining them all on leashes much like she had been when she walked with Master David.

Giving a hard yank, Shiva pulled the dragon and wolves out of their fight. They twisted, pulled, and tried to drain Shiva's strength. With the will and power of three demi-wolves and a dragon fighting against her, Shiva felt herself start to slip.

"*What are you doing, Shiva?*" Myst demanded. "*Help me get away from her!*"

"*Don't listen to her,*" Rocket insisted. "*You know she's bad! Help me stop her!*"

Shiva decided to focus on Rocket, as she was the strongest. *"Rocket, do you understand what the humans did? Do you know why Myst killed them?"*

Rocket wrenched her head, her mind batting aside the memories Shiva received from Luke. *"Who cares?"* her thoughts screamed. *"They were humans. Humans are all innocent. We don't kill the innocents."*

Myst chuckled darkly. *"You naïve fool,"* Myst growled. *"There's no such thing as an 'innocent' human. They're all despicable creatures. Selfish, entitled, miserable little bullies. They took advantage of the dogs who trusted and loved them!"*

"Well… that's not completely true…" Darius started to note.

But his protests were cut off; Shiva shuddered as disgusting visions filled the link between their minds; *of humans abusing animals, the land, each other.* They oozed through her mind like a river of oil, causing Rocket to scream as they were forced into her own mind.

"No!" Rocket insisted. *"Humans… have… good in them!"*

Rocket fought back with fiery vengeance. Shiva whimpered as Rocket's memories shot bright and hot across her mind: *humans helping each other. Caring for animals. Caring for her.*

The two memories swirled and wrestled with each other, using Shiva's head as the battleground. Shiva fell to her knees, groaning as the memories battled within her mind. Faintly, she heard a voice.

"Stop it!" Luke's voice demanded. "Stop it, you're hurting her!"

Rocket whirled on Luke with a snarl. Fire built at the back of her throat. Just before she could bathe the male in flames, Myst lunged at her, knocking her off course.

The links gave one final yank, throwing Shiva to the ground. She was forced to cancel them out, as Luke and Darius rushed to help Myst.

Shiva looked up in horror as the demi-wolves and dragon fought; Myst and her pack running circles around Rocket, carving through her scales while Rocket set their fur on fire.

Shiva had to stop this. She had to make them stop! Myst was mistaken about humanity, and Shiva had a very nerve-wracking feeling that each of them held only their small perspective of a much greater story. Beyond that, Luke demonstrated a care for her that no one had. She couldn't let Rocket hurt him when he clearly had good in him. She lifted a claw, summoning her pack link to intervene…

Only for a boot to grind into her back. She spun; Rider Buck stood over her, a mixture of malice and triumph shining on his face.

"I knew it," he said. "I knew you were still on her side." He lifted his boot to crush her head.

But Shiva rolled, dodging his strike. "No, listen…!" she tried to say.

Buck caught her with a kick to the nose. She tumbled backward as he bore down on her.

"No more lies," he snarled. "No more talk." Another kick to her ribs sent her rolling. "I'm ending this, right now!"

Growling in frustration, Shiva lashed out, catching his legs and pulling him off his feet.
His back hit the ground, and Shiva turned back to the demi-wolf/dragon fight. She tried to send her pack link, desperate to make them stop.

But Buck didn't stop. He didn't give up. Shiva's ear flicked as he approached, and she dodged backward, barely avoiding his punch. Another punch grazed her jaw, and she bit down on his arm, just as his free arm locked around her neck. Exhaustion pulled on her limbs, but she forced her muscles to feed on the adrenaline. Her pack link activated, twining and binding his limbs. Shiva felt a surge of energy enter her muscles. Meanwhile, Buck's knees buckled and weakened, the triumph faded from his eyes.

"N-No!" he stammered, as his skin paled as he slumped in Shiva's pack-link grip. "NO!"

But Shiva had no time for his games. She heard Luke yelp in pain. Saw Darius tumble. Rocket's red scales were a darker red than before. Her scales were cut and disjointed, and she was panting hard as Myst and Luke circled her.

Concentrating with all her might, Shiva lifted one of her claws and sent out a link. Her heart hammered as she saw Myst seize it.

"*Myst, stop…!*" Shiva tried to call.

But then Buck reached out and grabbed Shiva by the neck and slammed his head into hers.

Her link faded. He got her on her back. His grip around her neck tightened. He was going to overpower her! Focusing entirely on him, Shiva pulled every particle of strength she could get from him through the pack link. His legs gave out, and she rolled him onto the ground. She slammed his head into the ground. His grip loosened, but not enough.

I need more...

She slammed his head again. And again. Reluctantly, his hands released the iron grip from around her neck, but he shoved his arm deep into and out of her mouth, trying to disengage his arm by force and sheer will.

Instinct forced her to bite down harder; to tear into the flesh of his arm as she sucked the very life from his being.

He moaned in agony, his free hand slipping enough to wedge into her eye. Pain flared into her brain, and she smashed his head, again on instinct.

A sickening CRACK echoed. His entire body went limp. She tore herself free from his grip, spitting his broken arm out of her mouth with distaste.

And covered her mouth in horror.

Buck was eerily still. His skin was as pale as if the man were drained of all his blood. Foam bubbled out of his mouth, and his eyes stared without seeing. Where his head was smashed against the ground, a concave, inward curve of the skull became apparent. Blood oozed like oil from his scalp.

"BUCK!" Rocket screamed.

Shiva spun as Rocket rushed her. Shiva didn't hesitate, and sprinted away from Buck's body. She gave Rocket the room she needed as the dragon spread her wings and leaned over to protect her rider. Rocket trembled by Buck's side as she tended to him.

"Teeth-For-Days, please no…" Rocket whimpered, nursing Buck in her arms as she rocked his body back and forth. "Buck? Buck, can you hear me! Buck!"

Shiva was motionless from disbelief, watching as the dragon tended to her broken human. This wasn't supposed to happen. As Rocket held him tenderly in her talons, her electric green eyes lifted and locked on Shiva's brown orbs. Shiva shivered at the betrayal burning in Rocket's eyes.

"Why?" Rocket whispered. "I trusted you! I TRUSTED YOU!"

"Shiva!" Myst barked. "Lucifer, grab her!"

"It's Luke!" Luke's voice protested.

"Just grab her!"

A claw closed around Shiva's shoulder, and she was pulled away from the scene. But even as she was yanked into the shadows, she couldn't get the picture of those terrifying eyes out of her head. That broken, eerily still body.

Nor could she stop herself from hearing Rocket's venom-filled words.

"SHIVA! IF IT'S THE LAST THING I DO… I'll get you for this."

Chapter 6: Murderer

Shiva was certain Rocket would chase them to the ends of the earth. Nowhere would Shiva be safe from her wrath. As the demi-wolves shot through the thick underbrush and leaped over the dense roots dominating the forest, Shiva couldn't shake the memory of Rocket's eyes, or Rocket's vow of vengeance.

When Myst barked for the pack to stop, Shiva almost ignored her, wanting to run and run and run until she found her way back to her Master. She wanted to be where she could hide under Master David's bed covers and find some way to be safe. Safe from Rocket's horrifying eyes, and the terrible sound of Buck's head cracking on the ground.

Shiva had forgotten about Luke holding her claw until he slowed down. She lost her balance and stumbled, catching herself and looking up at Myst.

The sight caused Myst to chuckle, as she reached out and steadied Shiva.

"Easy there, Shiva," she said. "We're safe now; you're safe!"

Shiva wrenched herself out of Myst's grip. "Don't touch me!" she barked. Her power made her fur pulse. "Rocket's gonna get me! I killed Buck! I…"

"You did what you had to do," Myst insisted. She leaned in close, almost solicitous. "You did what you had to do."

"It's what we all have to do," Luke added.

Despite their words, Shiva couldn't shake the sight of Buck's fractured skull. The fire in Rocket's voice. The despair… the betrayal of trust…

The fear that she had done something seriously wrong.

Darius's voice snapped her back to reality.

"So… I know everyone's a little freaked out, but… what do we do next?"

"I don't know about you," Luke replied. "But I could use something to eat."

Shiva groaned, certain she would never eat again.

"How can you think of eating when we've got the Pack Link now?" Myst asked. "The dragons don't stand a chance against us anymore. We can finally take the fight to Drake himself!"

Myst's words grated on Shiva's ears. She put her claws to her ears, trying to block the wolves out. Shiva, her head lowering, saw the eyes *flashing before her. Rocket and Buck were right in front of her. She could feel Rocket's talons digging into her shoulders again.*

"Guys… HEY!" Luke boomed, pulling Shiva back to reality. She clung to him as he pulled her away from Myst. "I think Shiva's gone through too much today. She needs a chance to… oh, what's the word…?"

"Acclimate?" Darius asked.

"Can I fight that?" Luke asked, before shaking his head. "Argh, I mean… yeah. That."

Myst growled, but the males eyed Shiva's trembling presence with a worried air. They gave Myst concerned looks, and the Alpha finally relented.

"Fine," she muttered. "Give her some time to adjust." She turned to Darius. "Darius; come with me."

Darius grinned. "At least someone remembers my name ain't Derry," he mumbled.

"Just come on," Myst insisted. "I've got an assignment for you."

The demi-wolf followed obediently, while Luke guided Shiva to a more secluded spot.

"You're gonna be okay," Luke assured her. "First time's always the roughest, but it'll get easier. You'll be fine."

But... Shiva thought. *I don't feel fine. Honestly, I feel...*

Shiva gagged. Luke backed off and let Shiva fall to all fours, retching and coughing up bile; an unfortunate result of having nothing to eat since she was transformed.

"Shiva?" Luke barked, panicked.

"Lucifer, give her space," Myst warned, reappearing from the foliage.

"But..."

"I said give her space!" Myst barked harshly.

Reluctantly, Luke backed off. Shiva lifted her head, struggling not to retch again, and found Myst's golden eyes only a foot away from her own.

"You okay?" Myst asked, genuine concern in her voice.

Shiva shook her head. "No," she admitted. "No, I'm pretty far from okay."

"Show me what's troubling you," Myst encouraged, offering her claw. "The Pack Link can help, if you let it."

Without much choice, Shiva took Myst's claw, and watched as the lightning formed some kind of golden cocoon around their entwined claws.

Shiva felt herself slipping away, almost like she was flowing into a river of air. Rocket's eyes flashed before her again, cradling Buck's broken form.

"*I trusted you,*" hissed in her ears.

But worst of all was the image of Buck. The sight of him broken. His skull caved in like a broken eggshell. Briefly, his form flickered – and Shiva's heart raced twice as fast as she saw David in Buck's place. Just as dead. Just as broken.

Myst's voice scoffed. "You're worried about the human?" she asked.

"He was Rocket's master," Shiva insisted. "She has every right to want revenge against me. W-What if she killed my master?"

Myst's grip on Shiva's claw tightened.

"You have no master," Myst murmured darkly. "We are the masters of our own fate. That's what you and I are here for."

A vision flashed before Shiva's eyes – *her and Myst standing over a destroyed Walls of Cadmus. Claws raised, snouts held high. Echoing back a howl, as thousands of demi-wolves howled below them. Covering the city, with the humans nowhere to be seen.*

"Power to the canines," Myst declared. "Something the humans would have you forget!"

"But…" Shiva protested. "One of them cared for me."

Her memories shifted again. *She saw herself as a puppy, covered in snow and half frozen to death, when David found her. He picked her up and cradled her in his arms like a father with his newborn child. She could still feel the warmth of his chest.*

But the memory was broken by Myst's laugh.

"You honestly thought he cared for you?" Myst demanded. "He wanted to use you."

Shiva's memories were pulled forward: her hunting for David; finding squirrels and rabbits and being his shoulder to cry on. And yet, they seemed… different. David didn't usually take the prey Shiva caught with that much force. He didn't hold Shiva like he was trying to strangle her.

"I'll give you this, though," Myst noted. "He was one of the nicer ones."

New memories surged into Shiva's brain. Memories that made her scream.

Myst was chained down on a table in a dark room. A man festooned in the shadows – Luco, Shiva remembered from the arena – showing her photos.

Dogs trapped in cages. Dogs laid out on tables and stuck with syringes. Scalpels digging into their bodies without anesthetic, sometimes as the canines begged for mercy.

Ugly-looking humans tugging dogs on leashes that were more like nooses. Leaving them out in cold and damp backyards, abandoned, soaked, thirsty and starved.

"This is what humans think of you," Luco whispered, pacing around Myst's bound form. "This is how they've always felt about you. You are just an object. A puppet. A tool to be used and discarded."

The snap of a whip sounded. The pain of a knife carved across Myst's back, the pain rebounding into Shiva's body.

"STOP IT!" Shiva wailed.

"Myst, enough!" Luke barked, jostling Shiva, tearing away the pack link and yanking her out of the violent thoughts.

Shiva clung to Luke, trying to anchor herself to some sort of reality, as her body trembled, and she struggled not to retch again. Myst gazed at her with sympathy.

"I wish it was different," Myst said. "Truly, I do."

She reached out a claw, but Shiva cowered away from it. Luke held her tighter, shaking his head at Myst. Reluctantly, Myst lowered her claw.

"There are too many bad humans in this world," Myst said. She looked away with a glower. "They've been dominant for far too long. It's made them think they can do whatever they want, without consequence; without retaliation."

Shiva looked at Myst's claws and noticed they were trembling. Myst caught her gaze, and clenched her claws with a shudder.

"As far as I'm concerned, you gave that beast exactly what he deserved," Myst said. "And the sooner you realize that… the better things will be for everyone."

Myst disappeared into the shadows.

Shiva watched her go, her grip on Luke not fading. Gently, the male demi-wolf eased her against a tree.

"I'm sorry about that," he mumbled. "Myst tends to get pretty… 'passionate'… when it comes to certain subjects." He hesitantly released her. "Can I… um… do you… need anything?"

Shiva glanced up at him, before silently nuzzling into his chest; taking comfort in knowing that at least one demi-wolf had her back. As he cuddled her, Shiva's pack link tied them together.

Shiva saw Luke staring at an abandoned series of cages, Myst next to him.

"What's all of this?" he asked.

"The humans called them dog pounds," Myst replied. Before she could explain what, they were…

"Can I fight those?" Luke asked.

Myst grimaced. "Well, not anymore…"

"Can I eat them?"

Myst scoffed. "I'd love to see you try."

Luke's ears perked up. "A challenge?!"

Myst's tail tucked. "What? No-no…!"

"VERY GOOD!" Before Myst could stop him, Luke lunged at the nearest cage, ready to take a bite out of the bars.

For the first time since the fight, Shiva chuckled. "Did you seriously…?"

"I seriously did," Luke replied with a wag of his tail. "Had to get my teeth fixed, but I showed her."

"Oh, my…" Shiva couldn't help but laugh. But Luke just laughed along with her.

Shiva started to explore his memories. The time where he tried to eat a redwood tree. A time when Darius, Myst, and five other demi-wolves were injured, and he carried all of them home on his back. A shocking memory where Luke got into a brawl with a bear over a deer leg, which he promptly gave to Darius.

Shiva was tempted to just lose herself in Luke's memories. Yet, in the back of each of them, she could still hear Myst; *her words flowing around his brain from countless lectures.*

"Humans are not to be trusted!" Myst told Luke. "They are cruel and heartless beings that see you as nothing but a slave. A puppet! A tool to be used and discarded."

"David wasn't like that," Shiva growled defiantly.

Instead of arguing, Luke tilted his head in intrigue. "*What did he do? What was he like?*" his voice asked.

In answer, Shiva gave her own memories of Master: *when her leg was caught in a hunter's bear trap, he not only carried her home, he made the trap's owner pay for her recovery. The time she managed to run down a deer, and he let her have the biggest share of the meat. Every time he would scowl and grumble about the 'idiots he had to call family,' only for his sour expression to fade into a sweet smile when he gazed upon Shiva.*

"You're all the family I need, Shiva," he said, patting her head. "Don't know what I'd do without you."

As his words echoed in her mind, Shiva's ears perked. What would he do without her?

"Luke?" she whispered.

"Yeah?"

She stared up into his blue eyes, hoping against hope he would understand.

"I need to go home."

His ears flicked. His head tilted in confusion.

"Where I came from," Shiva clarified. "I have to find my master."

For a moment, he was silent. His ears flattened in doubt. Shiva's heart beat faster, worrying he was going to say no. But as his eyes shone with the memories she showed him; watching the way David's face lit up when he saw Shiva, the big demi-wolf grinned.

"Okay."

Shiva straightened. "Y-You mean it?" she asked.

"Of course," Luke said with a scoff. "What kind of heartless beast could say no to that?"

Briefly, doubt stopped her. "Myst?"

"Oh, she'll understand," he replied. His grin widened as he took her claw, letting the pack link spark between their fur. "And with this?" He chuckled. "Who's gonna stop us?"

Shiva struggled not to laugh with glee. But then, out of the darkness, Rocket's voice growled. "I am."

Shiva's smile dropped. Her blood turned to ice in her veins. Her heart hammered against her rib cage.

Luke's eyes narrowed with determination.

"Link," he hissed.

Shiva's pack link spiraled into being, and Luke spun, catching the fireball that had been launched at Shiva's head.

Shiva tugged on the link, and the fireball drained into the lightning surrounding Luke's claws.

"MYST!" he howled.

"SHIVA!" Myst barked, lunging out of the foliage.

Darius didn't follow, but Shiva didn't have time to wonder where he was. Shiva projected a link to Myst, right as Rocket dodged past Luke's lunge and whacked Shiva into a tree with her tail.

Shiva tumbled into the tree, spots dancing before her eyes with searing pain, before the pain faded into the links.

Rocket roared, her rage distorting her words into an animalistic shriek. Luke and Myst caught her with the pack link lassos, but Rocket's body lit up in flames, and burned the links as if they were actual ropes.

For a moment, the demi-wolves circled the dragon. But her eyes didn't stray from Shiva. The white demi-wolf lay where she landed, fear locking her in place as Rocket roared again, this time with words Shiva understood.

"MURDERER!"

"*Murderer...*" the word bounced around in Shiva's brain. The vision returned: *Buck's broken body. Rocket futilely tending to him. The sorrow in her eyes. The rage.*

"*Shiva!*" Luke's voice barked in her head. "*Shiva, stay focused!*"

"*You did what you had to do,*" Myst insisted. "*She has no right to be angry at you for that!*"

Shiva shook her head. "*But she does,*" Shiva insisted. "She does..." she whispered out loud. She gazed up at Rocket with sorrow in her eyes. "Rocket, I'm so sorry."

"Does 'sorry' bring him back?" Rocket growled. "Does 'sorry' undo what you've done?" Her eyes shut, and steam hissed as tears streaked from her eyes; tears evaporated by the heat of her flames. "I trusted you!" Rocket seethed. "You said you wanted to help!"

"I-I did!" Shiva stammered. "But..."

"But nothing!" Myst barked, turning to Rocket. "Your rider was a tyrant and a thug. You deserve better than him!"

Rocket's voice cracked as she roared at Myst, only for Luke to jump on her back.

As the wolves and dragons fought, Shiva once again tried to make them stop. She sent a link out to Rocket, wanting to help her. Wanting to calm her down.

But she failed to spot the figure creeping up behind her. A bright glint reflected too late off of the light from Rocket's fire.

Luke briefly glanced back. Struggling against Rocket, he could do nothing more than bark. Before Shiva could discern the meaning in his panicked cries, an arm wrapped around her chin, yanking her head up and exposing her throat.

She felt a pinch on her neck, and wrenched herself free, spinning only to find a familiar woman standing before her.

Jericho.

An empty syringe in her hand.

Chapter 7: The Good Doctor

Shiva didn't know where she was anymore. Her entire body was numb, she couldn't feel her claws or her paws. Her vision had tunneled into a swirling vortex of blurring colors. Her heavy breathing drowned out the other noises.

A deluded part of her wondered if she had been blasted back in time: back to when she was just a regular puppy, being carried out of the snow by her Master David. She could feel his arms around her. The cold could explain why she felt so numb.

But… something was wrong. David was strong and powerful. This human was softer. Shiva could feel a bosom pressed against her neck instead of a muscular chest.

It took everything she had, but Shiva tried to focus her vision to see what was going on.

Another shock; there were several humans this time. Two of them were female, judging by their scent. She remembered Jericho's scent from the house.

The difference frightened Shiva, and she tried to squirm away with a whimper. When her limbs refused to obey her, she called on her powers. But even those only caused her fur to flicker like a dying ember.

One of the unfamiliar humans paused. "I think it's waking up," he whispered.

"She never fell asleep," Jericho replied. "It's an anesthetic; she'll be out of it for a while, but she'll recover."

"Well, can't you do something that'll keep her asleep?" another human demanded. "We can't risk her waking up; the dragon is still keeping those wolves busy."

#

Back at the clearing, Rocket had planted herself between the demi-wolves and the humans who had taken Shiva. Though the pack link had long since failed, Myst and Luke fought to go after the humans. Rocket fought back with equal ferocity, distracting them from their pursuit, and giving the humans a chance to get away with Shiva in tow.

Yet, as she fought, Rocket smiled inwardly. *"Don't think this is over, Shiva,"* she thought to herself. *"I'm still coming after you. One way or another, you're gonna pay."*

#

The thought of Rocket sent another frightened whimper out of Shiva. Another pulse of light.

"S-Seriously, do something about that light!" the scared human insisted.

"I can't; what if the mixture hurts her!" Jericho refuted.

"We can always dissect the corpse!"

Shiva's breathing sped up. Her claws shifted, lifting to defend herself. But Jericho gently took her claws and rested them on her shoulders.

"It's okay," she whispered. "I'm not gonna let anything happen to you again."

Shiva's eyes slid shut. She felt her fur pulse one last time with light. Little white tendrils wrapped around Jericho's fingers as Shiva slipped from consciousness.

#

In Shiva's dream, she saw Jericho with a dog. A beautiful cinnamon brown greyhound. She was a stray dog that Jericho had found – with a broken leg and covered in ticks - deserted behind the dumpster of the veterinary clinic at which she worked.

Other memories flashed within the vision. A paper with the headline 'Dogs turn on us; Man's Best Friend now Man's Worst Enemy!' Images of humans who had lost their lives to the canines.

Yet, as Jericho found this one dog, she didn't see a malicious monster. She saw a scared pup. So slowly, carefully, Jericho gained her trust. She left meat and water for her near the dumpster, and guarded her while she ate. She named the dog 'Lizzie,' and spoke to her with soothing words; inviting her forward with gentle offers of her hand. When the day came that Lizzie trusted her enough to inch out from under the dumpster and let Jericho touch her, she brought the little stray into the clinic.

She got rid of the ticks. She fixed her broken leg and gave the girl a bath.

And yet… others looked at Jericho like she was crazy.

"You know how dangerous dogs are now, right?" they demanded.

But Jericho… Shiva found her tail wagging. *Jericho was like David. She didn't care. When Lizzie sat on Jericho's lap, despite being far too big, Jericho rolled with it and scratched her ears all the same. Jericho took Lizzie to her clinic and encouraged others to* pet her, so that they could see for themselves that dogs weren't so bad. There was true love in Jericho's eyes, and there was love in Lizzie's eyes. They were a family.

But then the day came when another woman came to Jericho's door. Unlike Jericho, this woman didn't smile.

"You have a dog on you," the woman insisted. "By order of Cadmus, you must turn it over."

Just like David, Jericho refused with force. But she also knew they would return. She took Lizzie out into the woods. She cupped her head in her hands.

"I'll be right back," Jericho promised the dog.

She returned to her home. She feigned ignorance when the woman returned, this time with backup and once again demanding the dog. She let her search the house, but Jericho had already hidden all evidence of Lizzie's presence. When the woman was forced to leave without her prize, Jericho eagerly sped off to the woods to retrieve her friend.

"Lizzie!" she called. "Lizzie?!"

But Lizzie didn't answer. There was no bark, or whine.

Instead, the response came in a voice she didn't recognize; speaking in a language she didn't understand.

Then she found her.

Myst. Standing over Lizzie, and some random human. Myst held a book in one claw, and her other claw was held over the dog and human. White energy gathered around Myst's claws as she chanted the incantation.

"Hey!" Jericho yelled. "What are you doing?"

But Myst's eyes locked with Jericho's, and Jericho froze at the sight. Glittering golden orbs, alight with a fury the doctor couldn't understand. Then the power flashed. Jericho was flung back, and when she stared at her beloved Lizzie… she was now a demi-wolf.

But only for so long. As Jericho tried to approach, Myst dragged Lizzie into the shadows. When Jericho pursued… the vision shifted to reveal flames burning down an entire town. A dragon flying away, and Jericho falling to her knees before Lizzie; the former dog scorched and eerily, disturbingly still.

At first, Jericho directed her anger at Myst. She began to track the movements of the new demi-wolves. As Jericho tracked her cases, she noticed that the only humans Myst pursued were... abusers. These were budding sociopaths hurting household pets, or owners who had mistreated their charges. Each was found with some evidence of their crimes resting next to their remains. Each had the same message written in blood. "Who's the Real Beast?"

The focus of Jericho's hunt shifted. It wasn't about vengeance anymore. It was about trying to understand. Onward, past villages and towns, she was relentless in tracking down the one called 'Myst.' Jericho was trying to discover why she was doing this, and why she had taken Lizzie.

Eventually, she found her. It was almost like Myst wanted Jericho to find her. She set the stage in the ruins of an old facility. Myst was standing triumphantly before a selection of skulls on spikes. Myst's eyes glittered maliciously at Jericho as she approached.

"Why'd you do it?" Jericho asked. "Why'd you take Lizzie from me?"

"You fascinate me," Myst noted to Jericho, her tone affable yet cold. She pointed at one of the skulls behind her. "This man *systematically slaughtered lives for 'taking up space.' And yet, because they were stray dogs... I'm the murderer?"*

"Of course not," Jericho said. *But before she could find a way to refute her, Myst had already moved on to another victim.*

"This woman took newborn children away from their mother," Myst continued. *"And yet, because the mother and children were dogs, I'm the monster?"*

"You're not taking into account!" Jericho tried to say, before Myst pointed to another skull.

"This one fought to have a poor, struggling life extinguished for the crime of self-defense," Myst growled. *"And yet, because that life belonged to a canine, the human's the only one that gets a memorial?!"*

"I wasn't like that," Jericho said firmly. *"I loved Lizzie. She was family."*

"Family?" Myst mused with a chuckle. *"That was the deal, wasn't it? When the first wolves came to your fires? We protected your homes, and in exchange, we were to be treated like family."*

She ripped her mask off, and Jericho's breath hitched as she beheld what lay underneath. Shiva couldn't believe it. *Someone had* seared an image of a skull onto Myst's forehead, and flame patterns along her snout. Though the pattern might have worked as war paint, someone had chosen instead to carve the patterns into her flesh. Myst pointed at the scars, her eyes glittering in rage.

"Is this how you treat family?!'" Myst boomed.

"I…" Jericho whimpered, backing up. "I didn't…"

"No," Myst agreed. "You don't know. Because you don't have to know. Because we can't tell you. And because we can't tell you, 'no' or 'enough,' that entitles humans to treat us however they want, right?"

"I-It's not like that!" Jericho whispered.

Myst's eyes glittered, and she re-donned her mask.

"Your actions speak a lot louder than your words," she said, drawing her claws. "But I'll give it a shot; I'll say, 'No!'"

"Myst…" Jericho pleaded, backing up as the wolf moved toward her. Behind her, Shiva thought she saw a familiar scaled bird, dropping down from the air.

"I'll say 'enough!'" Myst growled, unaware of the approaching dragon. "And one way or another, you're all going to listen!"

"Please!" Jericho screamed.

But as Myst lunged at Jericho – at Shiva – the dragon moved to intercept... and Shiva snapped out of the vision.

She found herself in a padded cell. Soft, white padding covered the small room, with the exception of a single glass window. Her limbs were no longer numb, and she heard voices from the other side of the window. Jericho's voice, along with the scared, unfamiliar human. Shiva raced to the window, and sure enough, Jericho was there talking with another woman with snow-white hair that contrasted sharply with her young, smooth features.

"It had something bound to you!" the voice of the unfamiliar human insisted. "Some kind of white light! It was probably trying to rip your hand off or something!"

"Is my hand gone?" Jericho asked, showing her uninjured hand to her companion. "This one wasn't doing anything! I didn't even notice it was there!"

"You're too soft on these animals."

Jericho glanced at Shiva with a grin. "We'll see. David Johnson said that Myst wouldn't turn this dog. If we're lucky, he was right." She turned to Shiva before she could speak. "Now, just hang on a second there, ma'am. We're going to get this sorted out, just give me some time."

David! Master! Shiva alerted on his name, even as Jericho escorted her companion away. Questions fought against fear in her mind. Where was he? Was he safe? What had that vision been about? More importantly, what was Jericho going to do with her, now that she finally had her?

Shiva wasn't sure. And she had a sinking feeling that she wasn't going to like it when she found out.

"It's your own fault, you know?" a voice in her head noted – eerily similar to Rocket. *"Murderer."*

Buck's broken body flashed through her mind once more, but... then it was accompanied by memories of the arena. His glower had never left her. He was perpetually looking for an excuse to attack her.

"He wasn't exactly a saint either," another voice argued – similar to Myst's. *"Why should he be allowed to hurt and abuse us, and have us feel guilty for fighting back?"*

His memories answered; what he had lost to Myst. His village. That woman.

Shiva grimaced in frustration. Buck may have been violent and cruel, but Shiva answered his violence with anger and hate of her own. Look where it had gotten her; locked up in some mysterious prison, awaiting torment from another person who thought they were justified because she was a demi-wolf.

"*Well, not this time,*" Shiva decided. When Jericho came back, no matter what her intentions were, Shiva would refuse to give her another excuse to see her as something to be feared. "*I will make you see me for who I am,*" Shiva promised. "*I don't know how just yet, but it definitely won't be through force and violence. I am NOT a monster.*"

She lowered her head, that thought circling her mind as she waited for the humans to return.

"*I'm not a monster. And I'll prove it… somehow.*"

Chapter 8: The Interrogation

When the humans returned, Shiva was ready. She waited at the back of the cell, her head held high with her claws behind her back.

The same two humans returned: Jericho and the second one; a pale, white-haired woman with intimidating glacier blue eyes. They stepped over the threshold, taking care not to make any sudden movements. For a moment, the demi-wolf and humans regarded each other.

The white-haired woman glared at Shiva with suspicion, like at any moment, the demi-wolf might attack them. Jericho was more cautious, like she was trying to discern whether Shiva was a demi-wolf or some kind of jewel.

"So, um…" Jericho began hesitantly. "Hello."

Jericho's companion glanced at her fellow human with a raised eyebrow. "Hello?"

"It's important to start somewhere," Jericho hissed back, before smiling at Shiva. "My name's Jericho. Evelyn Jericho."

"We've met," Shiva replied neutrally.

Jericho nodded, her head bowing. "Aye," she admitted. "I'm sorry about what happened to your Master, and for scaring you. But... I thought I could help you. Maybe we can still help each other now." She indicated her companion. "This is Regina Winters."

"The one trying to make sure the dog lover over here," Winters gestured to Jericho, "doesn't get killed."

Shiva glanced at Jericho before replying, "Well, my name is Shiva," careful to keep her voice calm and neutral. *"See, not a monster. I can show you that."*

Jericho glanced at Winters, grinning with triumph, while Winters merely rolled her eyes before glancing cautiously at Shiva's claws.

"Well... 'Shiva,'" Jericho began, pulling in a chair from the outside. "I can imagine this is all just as confusing for you as it is for us." She indicated her chair. "Can I sit?"

Shiva smiled wryly and nodded. "Make yourself comfortable. I'd bring you refreshments, but..." she indicated the cell.

Winters narrowed her eyes.

"Regina..." Jericho warned.

"I'm not doing anything," Winters gave Shiva a hard stare. "As long as you don't try anything."

Jericho sighed and smiled at Shiva. "Please, forgive my partner. she's gotten rather suspicious after meeting other demi-wolves before you."

"Suspicious?" Winters laughed humorlessly. "Did you not see this thing crack open a dragon rider's skull like a watermelon? Did you not see what Myst did to our government?"

Indignation and fury rose up in Shiva's gut, but she forced the emotions down. *Getting angry at these two isn't going to help anything,* she reminded herself. *I've got to make a good case for why that was a mistake.*

"I am more focused on how 'this' demi-wolf connects to the other demi-wolves with tendrils of light," Jericho replied, turning to Shiva. "Care to tell us about that?"

Shiva's ears perked. "You saw that?" she asked.

"We've had eyes on you ever since you went near the Walls of Cadmus," Winters replied. "Now answer the question."

Shiva swallowed, once again finding herself in the same situation as she had with the dragons. The Pack Link was her only real power. Letting them know about it could lead to countermeasures from them later. But, at the same time, this was about earning trust, so… Shiva took a breath and spoke.

"It's called the Pack Link," she replied, letting her fur glow. "It was conceived by Myst as a way to give demi-wolves an advantage over the dragons."

Jericho smiled softly. "I always knew that Myst was a smart one…" she whispered.

"But what does it do?" Winters asked, her eyes still stern but softer. Curious. "The dragons are our only real defense against your kind. How does it get past them?"

Shiva chuckled, before looking to Jericho. "You remember those threads that I had wrapped around your wrist when you brought me here?"

Jericho looked down at her hands, Winters giving her a shocked look.

"What did you do to her?" Winters asked.

"Nothing," Shiva assured quickly. "I just saw her memories." She looked at Jericho. "I saw Lizzie."

Jericho winced, looking down as Winters glanced at her.

"Lizzie?" she asked, turning to Jericho. "Your dog?"

Jericho nodded sadly.

"You were so angry at Myst at first," Shiva whispered. "You felt like she took your daughter. But when you confronted Myst… and she asked, 'is this how you treat family'…"

Jericho paled and shuddered at the memory.

"… you had a hard time blaming her," Shiva finished.

Winters stepped back, her hands resting on a line of throwing stars on her belt. "And… what about me?" she asked, though her voice stayed level. "Did you get inside my head?"

"No," Shiva replied quickly. "My links need to touch you before any information or memories become apparent." Her heart thumped at the thought of adding more, but the expression of hope on Jericho's face drove her forward. "A-And anyone that links with me can use my power."

Jericho's eyes widened. "That's why the demi-wolves were able to fight like that."

"And why they stopped when the rider snuck up on her," Winters added, rubbing at her chin with a ponderous grin. "So, in essence…" she looked back at Shiva, "Whoever controls you controls the Pack Link."

Shiva swallowed. She didn't like the look in Winters' eye. "I-I'm not sure," she back tracked. "Myst didn't exactly train me in its use."

Jericho's brow furrowed. "Myst didn't train you?"

Shiva shrugged. "Well, Rocket didn't give her the chance."

With Jericho's rapt attention, Shiva retold her story, from the point where she and her master were attacked to waking up with Myst to the dragons finding her. Shiva spilled everything she knew, feeling a strange relief as she relayed her fear, her confusion, her suspicion, and her theories.

And to make matters better, the humans just listened: Jericho was captivated, and Winters stayed respectfully silent.

As Shiva told Jericho of her love for David, and her resentment towards Myst for thrusting her into this war, Jericho's eyes brightened. Shiva wondered if her words were reigniting the doctor's hopes; making her think that peace between demi-wolves and humans could be achieved. But she couldn't be sure until she finished.

Or so she thought. When she reached the part where she, Rocket and Buck went to the Walls of Cadmus, Winters interrupted.

"That was Myst attacking us," Winters noted. "Not that she could've gotten through, but your assistance was very good for morale."

"Or rather, Rocket was," Shiva corrected. "Since she protects you."

Jericho's gaze darkened. "She may protect us, but she does not speak for us. There are still plenty of us…"

"One of us," Winters muttered.

"…that remember dogs as Man's Best Friend," Jericho insisted.

"Though it's hard to see why," Winters said, turning to Shiva. "You know that, right? You said Rocket showed you what Myst did to us."

"Myst showed me what humans did too," Shiva admitted. "I don't know who to believe."

Jericho sighed. "The truth is," she admitted. "Humans aren't saints."

"That doesn't mean Myst is justified in relentless slaughter," Winters insisted.

Jericho glanced at Shiva. "Maybe it's something you could help us with."

Shiva's ears flattened. "Begging your pardon, but I tried. I tried to work with Rocket, and…".

"I'm not talking about working with Rocket," Jericho replied. "Rocket's too naïve, and the riders will want everyone to believe you're just a beast."

Shiva winced, remembering how open Rocket had been before Buck's death, and how Buck had never trusted her.

"I believe we can use you for something better," Jericho continued.

Shiva tilted her head. "Would that… 'something better' involve not killing me? Maybe letting me see David again?"

Winters chuckled, but Jericho just smiled.

"More than that," Jericho promised. "You could reunite other dogs with their masters as well."

Winters scoffed. "Brace yourself," she muttered.

But Shiva quickly forgot about Winters, as Jericho took her claws.

"Ever since Myst started her campaign of terror," Jericho said. "Dogs have been blacklisted by humans and dragons alike. Not all of them share Myst's mindset, but they've been forced to her side, because dragons and humans automatically think they'll join her if left to their own devices."

"So... self-fulfilling prophecy," Shiva guessed. Jericho chuckled darkly.

"Correct. Your master and Rocket? Well, I'm sorry to say, but they are part of a very small minority that seems to get even smaller by the day."

"With good reason," Winters interjected. "I know how you feel about the demi-wolves, Jericho. But we just can't trust them."

"We can trust her," Jericho insisted, nodding at Shiva before turning back to her. "And you can trust us, Shiva. With this power... maybe there's a way that we can identify which demi-wolves are still good, and which ones have been fully indoctrinated. Or even better..." Jericho's grip tightened. "Maybe there's a way we can show them that not all humans are the monsters that Myst and her loyalists make us out to be."

Shiva grimaced, part of her remembering what Myst went through; what Luco had done to her. But she didn't dare speak of it and tried to block her thoughts on it. Right now, she had Jericho's trust, which she could not afford to lose. Luckily, Jericho seemed too wrapped up in her grand delusion to notice Shiva's doubts.

"Shiva," Jericho insisted. "You could finally be the key to ending this war." She looked down. "We could save thousands of other dogs like Lizzie."

Shiva smiled.

"I'll do it," she said. "Whatever shows the humans and dragons that we're more than what they believe or have been brainwashed to believe."

Jericho released Shiva's claws, cupping her mouth in delight, before turning back to Winters. "Regina, go get the King. He needs to know about this."

Winters grinned. "Can I assume you'll be staying here with your new buddy?" she asked.

"Are you kidding?" Jericho asked. "I am not letting anything get in the way of this discovery." She put her hands together. "I understand that you have gone through some things; you and everyone else. But by God above, if I have a chance to save a dog I will. I couldn't save Lizzie… but I'll take her to the King myself if I have to!"

"NO-NO!" Winters said quickly, getting between the two. "Calm down, Jericho. I'll get the King. Just…" She glanced between the two again. "Don't do anything weird while I'm gone."

Jericho nodded, trying to resist bouncing on her heels like a giddy schoolgirl. Winters gave Shiva a stern glare.

"And you," she added darkly. "Don't take advantage of her."

Stamping down her indignation, Shiva opted for a nod. Luckily, she had an easier time of it, her tail wagging in equal excitement with Jericho's enthusiasm.

Here was someone who trusted her. Who believed she was good; that she wasn't just some mindless beast! Granted, Shiva had no idea how she could stop a war. But it hardly mattered; here was someone who saw her for who she was. And with luck, Jericho would reunite her with her Master. If the other dogs were to reunite with kind masters of their own… then why shouldn't Shiva go along with this plan?

Unfortunately, there wasn't much left to do after Winters left. As Jericho and Shiva were left alone, Shiva glanced around the cell.

"So… since we're on the same side," she noted, tapping the padding. "Think we can walk out of here?"

Jericho glanced at the cell walls, before chuckling. "Sorry," she said. "But it might be better for you to stay in here until the King's gotten to talk to you personally." She lifted her hands. "Don't get me wrong, he's a good man – he's been letting me look for demi-wolves like you in secret – but, everyone's gotta be a lot more cautious nowadays."

Shiva hummed softly. "I wish it didn't have to be like that," she admitted. "I wish you could know that I mean no harm; that you can trust me."

Jericho smiled, crossing over to Shiva and brushing the fur along her ear. "We'll change it," she promised. "You and me; we'll bring things back to the way they were."

Shiva grinned, and leaned her head into Jericho's stroking. For a while, they sat there in the cell, Jericho stroking Shiva just like her own Master used to; waiting for the King.

All too soon, they heard it; a *tap-tap-tap* of feet on the floor. Jericho got up excited.

"That must be him right now," Jericho said gleefully, practically skipping out the door. Shiva made herself stand up straight, holding her head high. She took a breath, ready to show the King what she had shown Jericho.

But as Jericho opened the door and stepped out, her eyes shining with hope… she was yanked away screaming. And Rocket stepped into view.

Shiva's tail tucked. Her smile faded. "Rocket?" she whimpered, shrinking back against the wall.

"I promised you, didn't I?" Rocket growled, tongues of flame licking at her teeth. "I told you, if it was the last thing I did… I'd pay you back for what you did to Buck."

"Stop! Don't!" Jericho protested, but Rocket's tail swished her out of the way.

"I didn't want to hurt him," Shiva insisted. "He wouldn't let me go. Rocket, please, you have to…"

But Rocket wasn't listening. She reared her head up, fangs glittering in the light of her fire. Pure instinct flowed through Shiva's heart, and she leaped to the side; barely dodging as Rocket's fireball went past her body and right through the wall.

The wall collapsed, revealing another stone corridor. And with an angry dragon roaring in rage behind her, Shiva did the only thing she could. She ran.

Chapter 9: The King

Where's the exit? Shiva thought, sprinting as fast as she could with Rocket's roar echoing behind her. *How do I get out of here?!*

Doors were located at fixed intervals, but every open door she turned to was just a cell similar to the one she just left. Some were empty, some held humans. But all of them had one thing in common: they were useless for trying to make an escape.

And she needed to make an escape fast. Rocket roared behind her, and as Shiva desperately tried to stay out of view, she could hear the dragon smashing and crashing through the concrete corridors that held her, forging a path through passages that weren't built for her bulk or size.

"I'm dead if she gets me," Shiva thought. *"Whether I deserve it or not, I can't let her catch me!"*

Her powers flared to life, covering her in spidery threads. A thought occurred to her.

Briefly, she stopped. Her heart swelled in terror as Rocket's clattering, lumbering movements drew near. But Shiva stood ready.

Soon, the red dragon rounded the corner. Her eyes contracted to thin slits of rage. As she moved to attack Shiva, the white wolf fired her pack links right down Rocket's throat.

The dragon gagged and grabbed at the threads, but Shiva drew the fire from inside Rocket. With a roar of her own, Shiva used Rocket's power to pummel through the wall… and into what she at first thought was a forest of steel.

She realized this was the city that lay beyond the Walls of Cadmus. The gray buildings stretched like trees – higher than any tree she had known. The buildings were covered with ceiling to floor windows, and even now, Shiva saw humans peering out of the buildings, their eyes wide with panic as they realized just what Shiva was.

"Did that wolf just bust out of jail?" someone demand.

"Where's that dragon? What is it doing?" another whimpered.

"It better do something fast," another person shrieked. "I don't want to take that thing on."

Shiva ignored the humans, desperately looking for an exit. For the most part, the buildings were laid out in a grid pattern, separated only by small alleyways or black roads. In one direction, one of the walls surrounding Cadmus rose up before her, while in the other direction, lay a building shaped like a rectangle with a domed roof that matched the wall in height.

In front of the domed roof building were two humans in armor, aiming boom sticks at her, just like David's.

"Is that a demi-wolf?" one of them asked. "Inside Cadmus?"

"Where's that dragon? How did that wolf get in?" the other demanded.

"DRAGON!" the first one yelled.

Shiva backed up, ready to try her luck with the wall. Rocket rolled out of the hole she had punched through the side of the building and rose up before her with a growl.

"Thanks," Rocket sneered. "You just made this easier for me."

Yet, as Rocket bore down on Shiva, the white wolf glanced behind her, and saw a furry form launch over the wall. It was Luke! Shiva didn't see Darius or Myst with him, but she realized he wasn't going to wait for them. Locking eyes with Shiva, Luke's massive form lunged from the top of the wall, careening toward Rocket like a furry cannonball.

Shiva didn't hesitate. She shot a pack link to him, not even caring when Rocket dodged.

"Not falling for that again," Rocket snarled, before her eyes dilated when she noticed Shiva looking at something behind her.

Before Rocket could follow Shiva's gaze, Luke – empowered by the pack link - crashed onto Rocket's back. Rocket roared in agony as Luke clawed her neck and snout. He turned back to Shiva.

"Get more power out of her," he said. "We can use the fire to fly out!"

Shiva readied another pack link, but not even a wolf landing on her was enough to dampen Rocket's fighting spirit. Throwing Luke off her with another roar, Rocket dodged the pack link and hit Shiva with a swipe of her tail. Shiva howled as she was flung through the air, flying in an arc towards the building with the domed roof. At the last second, Shiva thrust her claw out, sending a ball of fire that shattered the wall she was about to crash into. She tumbled into the building and rolled to a stop in an elaborately decorated hallway with a massive throne at the end of it.

Hitting hard and rolling off the ground, Shiva landed against the throne, tipping it over with a CRASH. She rolled back onto her paws and blinked at the downed throne in astonishment. Before she could fully regain her senses, the doors at the end of the hallway burst open, and armored humans ran in.

"W-Wait!" Shiva howled.

But her voice was drowned out by the screams around her: "Demi-wolf in the palace!"

Foregoing negotiations, Shiva ducked behind the fallen throne's seat, just in time to avoid a barrage of bullets that fired at her in a deafening salvo. Noticing a door behind her, Shiva called upon the last reserves of energy she had drawn from Rocket. She was able to send the throne flying at the coming guards as she turned to race through a doorway… only to stop cold when she found another human inside. He was seated in a chair with a table holding a glass of wine in one hand, and a smaller version of a boom stick or "rifle" in the other. The weapon was aimed at Shiva's chest.

A fresh wave of horror overtook her. The man in front of her didn't have armor like the others. Instead, he wore a flowing black robe that made it hard to tell how thin or muscular he was. A crown shaped like a hood concealed his pale face in shadows, but Shiva could still make out his teeth, shining in a grin like a crescent moon. His eyes glinted despite the darkness around his face, and his legs were crossed as if he was expecting her.

"Hello there," he greeted, in a frighteningly casual voice.

It can't be... Shiva thought. *Please don't let it be...* "Y-Your Majesty?"

The King's eyes glinted, and his smile widened. "Good. You know who I am," he replied.

It is! Shiva thought with horror. *I just barged into the territory of the King!*

Behind her, the guards poured into the room, guns clicking and clacking as they prepared to fire. Shiva lifted her arms with a groan and waited for the end. However, just before the guards could fire…

"Wait," the King commanded, lifting a hand.

"But sir," one of the guards said. "It's…"

"I said," the King said, his tone growing dark. "'Wait.'"

Reluctantly, the guards didn't fire. But Shiva could sense their tension. She could feel the muzzles pointed at her back.

However, she didn't dare to turn and look. She was trapped in the King's gaze. It astonished her how calm he was. He glanced down at his weapon.

"Can I put this down?" he asked. "I much prefer civilized discussions, which don't require firearms to be pleasant."

Shiva blinked in confusion, chancing a glance at the guards behind her. Taking that for an answer, the King set his pistol down, and exchanged it for the glass of wine.

"Thank you," he said, taking a sip of the concoction. "So," he continued, in that same conversational tone. "You're the demi-wolf that Jericho is so excited about? The one that's going to bring peace?"

"If it means I don't die, yeah," Shiva replied, flinching as one guard stepped behind her and angrily pressed his weapon between her shoulder blades. Her claws trembled in the air. "Please, your majesty, I know that Myst has done some horrible things, but I'm not on her side. I didn't even ask for Myst to come for me; she just kidnapped me!"

The King chuckled. "Yes, she is rather overzealous, isn't she?" he mused. His smile faded with a quiet sigh. "It's not a surprise the dragons are so scared of her."

"But I'm not like her!" Shiva insisted. "I'm not some violent killer o-or a terrorist! I'm just a girl who wants to get back to her Master."

The King hummed, taking a sip of his wine. Shiva's ears flattened and perked, waiting for his verdict.

"Well," the King replied. "Judging by how you didn't attack me the second you saw me and could have, I'm inclined to believe you."

Shiva pressed her claws together, her tail perking in hope. Hope that dwindled when he fixed a stern look upon her.

"However, I do have to ask about these rumors my guards have…concerning you," he noted. "Rumors involving the death of a certain Rider?"

Shiva winced, frustration mixing with resignation.

"I didn't want to do it," she said. "I was scared, and he wouldn't stop attacking me, and… I…" She looked up. "I know this looks awful, but I swear to you, I didn't want to hurt him! He gave me no choice!" Her ears perked, and she offered her claw, her pack link flickering to life. "And I can prove it."

The King tilted his head. He took another long sip of his wine.

"Careful, my king," one of the guards said. "You don't know what that thing can do!"

The King didn't reply, sipping his wine. He set the glass down, peering at Shiva's sparking claw like he wanted to examine it more closely with a magnifying glass.

But just as he started to reach his hand out…

"Your Majesty!" one of the guards yelled. "The dragon! Incoming!"

The King's eyes widened, and he looked behind Shiva with shock.

"Wait!" he called out. But it was too late.

"Please…" Shiva begged before a fiery hot talon closed over her head, cutting off her vision.

"Get away from the King, you *beast!*" Rocket snarled, hurling Shiva back into the throne room.

"STOP!" The King roared.

But with Rocket between him and her, Shiva knew it was pointless to try and continue the discussion. Spinning around, Shiva sprinted for the exit, but Rocket was faster and her back talons closed over her fur again.

"Not so fast," Rocket growled. "Let's take a flight."

With a cry of pain, Shiva was hurled out of the building, where her eyes met Luke's, who was desperately racing towards the palace.

Hoping against hope that he could help her, Shiva fired a link to him. But just as he seized her link, Rocket spotted the thread, and moved to intercept.

Shiva yelped, yanking her claws to her chest. But she felt a strange tug – something quite different from the times when Myst or Rocket tried to take her strength. The next thing she knew, Luke shot into the air, catching Rocket with a bite to the snout and knocking her off guard.

How did he…? Shiva stared at her link. *This thing can be used as a rope?!*

Seizing the stunned dragon, Luke's fur glowed red as Shiva's link pulled Rocket's fire into them. Summoning jets of flame from his back paws, Luke grabbed Shiva, detached from Rocket and in a single move, vaulted inconceivably high, nicking off a piece of the wall as they passed over the top and landing in the forest beyond.

Luke howled in victory, his joy spiraling through the link and into Shiva's veins like a drug. She went light-headed in his relief – his triumph – and howled in sync with him, too happy to worry about the King or Jericho or Rocket.

They were okay! Luke had saved her!

Sweet, strong Luke; who had just braved an entire city filled with soldiers and humans and dragons – just to help her.

For a split second, Shiva felt the urge to stop and stay entwined with Luke forever. But then a scream sounded. The two demi-wolves saw humans running toward them from the city gates. Luke's eyes narrowed, and he pulled Shiva toward the forest.

"Come on," Luke insisted. "Myst is waiting for us. Let's get outta here."

Nodding, Shiva made to follow him into the trees, when suddenly, a lone scream formed words that caught Shiva's attention.

"SHIVA, STOP!"

Shiva halted; it was Jericho's voice. Turning back, she saw the sympathetic human racing toward her. Right behind her, a battered and bruised Rocket cleared the wall. But before the dragon could charge…

"Everyone stop, please! I SAID STOP!" Jericho bellowed, coming to a halt and lifting her hands toward both Shiva and Rocket.

Rocket obeyed, banking in the air and landing in front of the guards. She stared at Jericho in frustration.

"You don't need to do this," Jericho insisted to Rocket. "Shiva's not the monster you think she is."

"She killed my Rider!" Rocket snarled. "Smashed his head open for…"

"And why do you think she did that?" Jericho shot back. "Because he attacked her, maybe? And why? What was she doing?"

"She must have been doing something!" Rocket insisted. "Buck wouldn't have attacked her without good reason!"

"Was that reason because she was just a demi-wolf?" Jericho exclaimed. "Just like how a human would kill another human for being different?"

Rocket paused. "Wait, what?" she stammered. "What are you talking about?"

"I won't deny that Myst has gone too far," Jericho admitted. "But this war wasn't started by her for no reason. Her fury and hate comes from the abuse she suffered at human hands. Just like the way Buck abused Shiva!"

"B-But... no!" Rocket insisted. "Buck was suspicious of Shiva. She..."

"Didn't. Do. Anything," Jericho said. "And if you're going to hurt her..." she stepped in front of Shiva and spread her arms wide. "Then you're going to have to hurt me too."

Luke's ears perked up in shock, while Rocket took a step back. Shiva's fur bristled, and she moved to Jericho's side.

"Jericho, no," she insisted. "You can't..."

"I can and I will," Jericho said, turning back to Shiva. "My dog was my best friend. I let myself believe they were all Man's Best Friend too." She lowered her head. "But I never thought about the humans who would break our bond... until it was too late." She looked back up at Rocket. "If this is what I have to do to repair our bond... then so be it. My life doesn't matter."

Rocket staggered. "No!" she insisted. "Your life does matter!"

"Just because I'm human?" Jericho asked with a humorless grin. "Myst is the way she is because some humans thought her life didn't matter. She was tortured and almost broken. Despite that, she survived. For once, see the value the demi-wolves have as living creatures… and leave Shiva alone."

Shiva gazed up at Rocket. She saw the doubt and sorrow in her eyes. The dragon looked away, almost towards her back, where Buck would've been sitting. But there was no Rider to tell her what to do. No Buck to give her advice.

In that moment, Rocket looked so lost and alone.

"I'm sorry," Shiva whispered, drawing the dragon's gaze. "I'm so sorry for what I did. I know it doesn't undo anything. I know it can't bring him back. But I'm really sorry."

For what felt like an eternity, Rocket and Shiva held each other's gaze. Shiva didn't need a pack link to see what Buck meant to Rocket; the adventures they shared. The days and hours they spent on missions and recreation. Rocket wasn't just some other creature.

She was Shiva, and Buck was her David. If Shiva had seen David ripped apart like that... what would she have done?

"Shiva," Jericho whispered, breaking her out of her trance. "Come back." She offered her hand. "Let's talk to the King."

"What?" Luke stammered. "But we just got out of there!"

"It's okay, Luke," Shiva assured him, smiling at Jericho. "This human can be trusted."

Jericho's expression brightened. Their hands almost touched.

Then Myst lunged out of the foliage.

Chapter 10: The Return

For a brief, shining moment, Shiva thought Myst had missed. She hit the ground, glaring at Rocket, Jericho blinking in alarm.

But then… thin lines of red began to spread slowly, darkly, murderously across Jericho's body. The human stumbled back, lifting her hands to her face. She tried to speak, but she only coughed up blood. Her body fell in slow motion. Legs crumpling, an arm reaching out, her head bouncing off the ground.

Shiva shrieked as if her master David were just hit. She lunged for Jericho, but Rocket and Luke were faster.

Luke yanked Shiva back, rolling out of the way as Rocket shot at them. Rocket's tail went wide, barely missing Myst as she dodged. The three demi-wolves backed up, Luke holding Shiva back as she desperately reached for Jericho. A pack link curled out, reaching for Jericho… only for Myst to catch the white tendril and hold it back.

"Evelyn!" Winters was screaming.

Rocket stood hunched over Jericho's body.

"Human," Rocket called to Winters. "Get your medics. Tell them there's a human down and you do it now!"

"Right!" Winters snarled, running back to the wall.

"Jericho…" Shiva sobbed, yearning for her with everything she had. But Luke's grip was strong, and he pulled her toward the forest.

"Myst," he said. "What do we do?"

Myst glanced back at Shiva. Her brow furrowed with despair. Back in the clearing, they could see the scene around Jericho. Rocket was distracted. They had to move.

"You stay with me, you hear?" Rocket hissed to the wounded human, her voice stern but gentle, as Jericho tried to gurgle out a response. "You're gonna live. I'm right here, just keep looking at me. I'm not losing another one."

Myst growled as she saw Rocket keeping pressure on Jericho's wounds, but reluctantly turned back from completing the kill.

"*Go back,*" Myst voice hissed through the link. "*As much as I want to, we can't fight them with Shiva like this. Rocket's* distracted, the humans did something to Shiva, and I intend to find out what."

Shiva snarled at Myst. 'The humans did something?' How could she think like that? How did she miss everything Jericho had just said? Shiva tried desperately to send out another link, but Myst caught it again.

"*Move!*" Myst barked.

Shiva fought Luke as he dragged her back into the forest, but with Myst controlling her links, there was little Shiva could do against their combined might. The last glimpse she had of Jericho was her moaning and gurgling on the ground, struggling to breathe as Rocket did her best to keep her alive. Briefly, she thought she saw Rocket look at Shiva. But her expression was unreadable, and the dragon quickly diverted her attention back to Jericho, hushing her and reassuring her until Shiva couldn't see or hear them anymore.

Even then, Shiva didn't stop resisting. Her pack link tied around Luke like an anaconda, her despair hitting him like rain.

"*Let me go!*" Shiva begged. "*I need to go back! Please, let me go back!*"

"*I can't do that!*" Luke insisted, as his own memories flooded her mind: *Rocket, ferociously fighting him; throwing Darius up against a tree like it was nothing.* "Rocket's too dangerous. We gotta leave while she's distracted!" He centered his thoughts on Darius. "*Speaking of...* where's Darius?" he asked Myst out loud.

"I sent him on another mission," Myst dismissed. "Anyway, we don't need to worry about him right now."

They ran for what seemed like an hour. Finally reaching a glade, Myst signaled Luke to stop. Grabbing Shiva out of Luke's grip, Myst confronted her.

"What is wrong with you?" Myst demanded. "Acting this pathetically over a human? And 'that' human in particular?"

"She was good!" Shiva choked out, the pack link spinning around them, *showing Jericho taking pity on Shiva. Promising her she'd see her master again.*

"She wanted to take you back," Myst insisted. "Just like she tried to take Lizzie back."

Shiva blinked, and in an instant, she saw the memory Jericho had shown her: Myst standing over Lizzie and the other woman. Performing the incantation that fused them.

"Stop!" Jericho's voice cried.

But... something was wrong. Jericho's face was alight, not with protective fear, but greed. From Myst's eyes, Jericho looked like a tyrant, demanding her property back.

"Lizzie was so much more than property," Myst insisted. "But they don't want to see that. That's why they sent the dragons, which ultimately killed Lizzie, and why they sent the dragons to try and kill me!"

Shiva saw the vision of Myst's meeting with Jericho again, the time when she had poured her heart out.

"You betrayed us!" Myst insisted. "Why? Because you could? Because we couldn't tell you 'no' or 'enough?'"

Jericho merely sneered at her, before glancing up. Myst followed her gaze, barely in time to avoid the fire from the dragon.

Shiva shook her head, overwhelmed. She tried to tear herself out of the link and backed up behind Luke, but Myst followed her, *sending forth visions of another arena.*

But unlike the one with the dragons, this arena was smaller. More compact. Only humans were watching. All of them cheering and jeering as Myst was forced to do battle with another wolf. The humans threw stones when the wolves hesitated and cheered louder and more boisterously when blood hit the ground.

"They see us as slaves!" Myst insisted, as Shiva struggled with the vision. "They think they have the right to treat us like objects! It's time for us to show them they're wrong! We matter just as much – if not more - than they do! The injustices they've foisted upon us can't stand!"

"But…" Shiva still valiantly protested, trying to hang on to the little sanity she felt she still had left. "Jericho regretted it. She wanted to fix it."

"She can't fix it!" Myst snapped. "None of them can fix it. There's too much evil in their hearts. They may be human, but they've lost their humanity!"

"That's not true!" Shiva insisted, pushing memories forward again: *David finding her in the snow. Taking her home. Rescuing her.* "David was good. He was kind! He loved me!"

"Loved you?" Myst almost laughed. "I saw him. He used you."

Shiva's memories were thrown back at her. *A glint in David's eye as he lifted her from the snow. Training her to hunt and run as soon as she could stand. Taking the prey she caught with a selfish gleam in his eye.*

Shiva wanted to protest, but a new fear gripped her heart. A terror unlike anything she had experienced yet.

"*I saw him.*" Myst had seen David? What did that mean?

Gripping the link, she let Myst's memories continue to flow. And her terror was realized:

Myst had seen David. Not just in terms of humanity, but she had seen him face to face. After she invaded his home.

In Myst's memories… Shiva saw herself, back when she was a normal dog. She saw herself being yanked into Myst's arms. And David, Myst's memories blurring his kind face into a grimace of irritation.

Rage colored Myst's memories a fiery red. She centered on the weapon in David's hands. The light in David's eyes that would defy and deprive Myst of his property. But Myst wouldn't let him deny this dog her freedom. She caught his weapon, redirecting it so the shot went wide. And before he could reload, she pulled him forward and slammed him next to an already unconscious Shiva.

Lightning spun around them as Myst hissed out a strange incantation. David screamed. And...

"NO!" Shiva howled, her link flaring out with the force of a bomb. Luke and Myst were flung from her, hitting the ground hard.

"Shiva!" Luke stammered, scrambling to his paws. "W-Wait... was that... but you said he was good!"

She barely heard him. *It can't be real! That wasn't real!* Shiva shook her head as Myst regained her paws.

"You didn't..." Shiva whispered. "I swear, you better not have!"

Myst merely glared at Shiva, her golden eyes narrowed in defiance. "He deserved what he got."

"If he deserved what he got..." Shiva whispered, her mind still trying to sort through situations where it turned out he was okay. Where he was alive.

But if he was alive...

Shiva spun and raced away. She closed her ears to the frantic howls of the demi-wolves. She focused her nose on finding home. Every ounce of energy she still had left in her, she devoted to getting back to her home as fast as she could.

And finding Master David.

#

The journey home took too long, in Shiva's eyes. Drinking from small streams and following water courses, she tried to erase the scent so the other demi-wolves couldn't track her.

Everything seemed to get in her way. Human bandits blocked her path for valuables she didn't have. Wild animals sought her flesh. A dragon and his Rider, hoping for the glory of beating a random demi-wolf.

But Shiva had no time for any of them. Thanks to her pack link, whenever an obstacle arose to stop her, she used the link to retaliate. Her pack link would drain the energy from whatever unlucky soul got in her way, leaving them prostrate on the ground, pale as a ghost, gazing in subdued shock as the white demi-wolf raced away from them.

Shiva didn't sleep, and rarely ate. During the few times exhaustion claimed her, she had horrible dreams of Myst maiming David in the most inhumane ways…taking him from this world and stealing Shiva away to be part of her unholy war against the humans and dragons.

But that didn't happen, her mind would cry out in defiance, wrenching her from the dream. *He's still alive! And I'm going to find him!*

Every once in a while, she heard Luke howl. *"Shiva,"* he called. *"I'm right behind you. Please, just wait for me!"* But Shiva didn't trust herself with him. Especially not with the devotion he showed to his Alpha.

She didn't know what to think, what to be, or who to trust anymore. All she could think about was getting back to David. Back to some semblance of the life she once had, before it had all been taken from her.

Her nose worked to her advantage; just like when she tracked elusive prey, the olfactory nerves now flirted with whiffs emerging and then disappearing of the scent of home. After what seemed like an eternity of non-stop, determined travel, she arrived.

Although, at first, it was hard to tell it was the same place. Moss, ivy, and wild kudzu vines claimed most of the home and outbuildings, and the few bits of wood left over from homes in the village served as nurse logs for wildflowers and honeysuckle. It was rather beautiful for what had become a graveyard.

No! Shiva thought furiously. *Not a graveyard. Master David is here. He'll be somewhere in here. I know it!*

Shiva shut her eyes, focusing on the scents at hand. Just like the times she invested herself in the scent of prey, she now focused on discerning Master David's scent. After a long moment of concentration, she was rewarded with his familiar musk.

It was faint; almost non-existent. But it was there, and Shiva pursued it like she would any other prey. Faintly, she heard the distant padding feet of Luke and Myst, but they could wait until later.

Myst will understand, Shiva thought with delusional glee. *Once she sees Master David, she'll never be able to deny; he was a saint. A wonderful man. A good man! She'll see… she has to see…*

Shiva followed the scent to her old home – a beautiful young oak sapling now stood in the ruins where the living room used to be. Scooting into the house, she searched through the debris for some sign that Master David had survived or perhaps wandered off somewhere else. Perhaps he had even carved out a home for himself here in the ruins.

Instead, she only found an ashen circle. A few bones – enough for two human feet and a dog's front paws – laying scattered around the circle, abandoned like trash. The scent trail hovered over the remains like a ghost, refusing to move beyond the circle.

Shiva's nose twitched. Where was David? Why was his scent leading, and then stopping her here? She sniffed around, but here is where the scent ended. The only direction it wafted from was the direction Shiva had just come.

"So," Luke murmured, creeping into the ruins to join her. "Is your master nearby?" He followed Shiva's gaze, his eyes widening as he beheld the ashy circle and bones. "Oh, no…"

"No," Shiva snapped. "NO! This isn't… that can't be…"

"Shiva… I…" Luke said quietly, lowering his head as Myst joined them, her eyes softening at Shiva's grief.

"Shiva?" she whispered. "You saw how the demi-wolves were made, right?"

Shiva remembered. She remembered they needed both a human and a wolf. But her denial of David's demise refused to allow her to connect the dots. Instead, it focused on the magic and what else the magic provided.

"W-Wait!" Shiva stammered. "T-The Pack Link. It takes powers, right… it can…" She turned to Luke desperately. "Can it take injuries too?"

"Well," Luke stammered, backing up, noting the panic in her eyes. "Yeah, it's supposed to, but…" He looked to Myst, who stepped forward apprehensively, but Shiva didn't have time for her.

Shiva blasted the bones with her pack link. Unfortunately, nothing happened. A few of metatarsals from the foot bones disintegrated into dust from the force of the link.

"Uh…" Luke grimaced as Shiva tried again. He looked to Myst. "The Pack Link can't connect to, uh… stuff that isn't alive, right?"

Myst shook her head. "Living creatures and plants, sure," Myst said. "But…"

"Curse it all, YOU'RE WRONG!" Shiva boomed, causing Luke and Myst to jump. "David can't die! David wouldn't just die like this!" She sunk to her haunches, the anger in her voice cracking into despair. "He wouldn't…"

Luke walked to her side, looking at her with sympathy. "Shiva?" he whispered.

Shiva covered her eyes, her claws digging into the sides of her head. "He can't..." she sobbed, looking up and howling. "Master? MASTER! MASTER!!!!"

Her wail and cries echoed off the trees, but the only response she got was from Luke.

"Shiva," he said solemnly. "He's gone."

Shiva gazed up at him, her ears flat and her tail tucked. His gentle – if blunt – words registered, and her mind finally accepted it. She fell forward onto his chest, howls of grief wracking her body as he rocked her gently back and forth.

"No..." she whimpered. "No-no-no..."

But her denial couldn't change reality. Master David was gone. And he was gone because Myst had used him to turn her into...

Myst had killed him.

Shiva's teeth bared. She looked past Luke to Myst, her head sympathetically bowed. At least, until she heard Shiva's growl.

"Shiva?" Luke asked, as she pulled herself free.

Myst looked up, blinking in alarm as Shiva advanced toward her. The white wolf's fur bristled, sparking with the pack link's power. A growl of fury rose from her throat.

"Shiva, what are you doing?" Myst asked. "Just think for a second: you're free now. You're not his slave! You're…"

But whatever Shiva was went up in lightning, as the white demi-wolf lunged for Myst's throat.

Chapter 11: Dog Fight

Shiva had had enough.

Once upon a time, she was happy and beloved by her master. Now, her home was destroyed, her master was dead, dragons and humans wanted her dead, and the only other creatures who gave her a chance to live were responsible for the loss of everything she loved.

Shiva was utterly done with this world. She was done with everyone who wanted her dead or wanted something from her. She. Was. Just. DONE. With. It. All!! And Myst was the perfect target for her unbridled rage.

With her mind utterly blank from the anger coursing through her, Shiva dedicated every ounce of her strength to reducing Myst to bones in the dirt, just as Master David was. She rushed at Myst, howling in rage as she slashed, shot electricity and bit. Her anger only became more inflamed when Myst dodged her strikes with relative ease.

"Shiva, stop!" Myst ordered. "He was just a human!"

"He was my Master!" Shiva howled, the pack link crackling around her like St. Elmo's Fire. "He was my friend!"

Shiva moved to strike, but she forgot about Luke. And his touch surprised her.

"Shiva," he begged. "She doesn't see them the way you do!"

Snarling, Shiva wrenched herself free. Like a gazelle, Myst leapt away, landing on a tree branch, just out of reach.

"Look at the bigger picture, Shiva," Myst insisted. "You lived as a slave under that human. Now you have the power to change everything!" She raised her claws and said softly, "I'm not going to fight you."

"Then you'll be easier to kill," Shiva growled, hurling a pack link like a spear. Fortunately for Myst, Luke shoulder-checked Shiva, causing the bolt to miss and blasting a chunk of a tree trunk away. Myst leapt clear of the branch. Shiva whirled on Luke, betrayal in her eyes.

"Myst isn't our enemy!" he insisted.

"She killed David!" Shiva countered. "She mutated us into monsters!"

"Not monsters…" Luke started to show her his memories.

But Shiva didn't have patience for equivocations. She slashed the pack link between them and raced after Myst as Luke gave chase.

"You took me from David," Shiva growled. "Dragged me into this war! And you think you're the hero here?"

She propelled her pack link tendrils forward again. But Myst caught the links. Reversing the power, she knocked Shiva back, both with her back paws and with a barrage of memories.

"How did she do that?" Shiva thought before the memories overtook her: memories of *grateful demi-wolves looking up to Myst. Taking their first shaky steps out of cages. Staring in awe at their vanquished abusers, as if unable to believe that humans could be defeated.*

"I saved our kind," Myst insisted. "I gave you the Pack Link to protect all of us. Do you think I wouldn't know how to battle you? Don't do this, Shiva!"

Shiva tried to counter with her own memories. But rather than remember her love for David, she remembered *the visceral fear of the arena, of seeing the dragon attack the demi-wolf.* "You caused this," Shiva growled darkly. "You didn't save us! You ruined our lives!"

With Shiva momentarily distracted, Myst barreled through the memories, and physically shoulder checked Shiva, sending her to the ground on her back.

"Only because the humans won't listen," Myst persisted. "How can I value their lives over our own when they don't do the same?"

#

Back at a hospital within the Walls of Cadmus, Rocket watched vigilantly as Jericho was brought back to life. Several surgeons surrounded her, and although the slashes Myst gouged into her were cauterized and no longer bleeding, Rocket's heart still fluttered at how still she was.

"Does she have a pulse?" Rocket asked, as Jericho was wheeled out of her grip. "Is she still breathing?!"

"We've got her from here," Winters replied. "You just focus on those demi-wolves."

"Yes," a low voice drawled. "And I'd rather you keep your rampant destruction 'outside' my city."

Rocket winced as she saw the King approach, with his hands behind his back. His frown was a frightful countenance, full of disappointment.

Rocket backed up. "Your Majesty… I'm…"

Winters held a hand up between them, blinking at something behind Rocket. "What… is that?"

Rocket followed her gaze: a thunderstorm was brewing on the horizon. Faintly, Rocket heard a howl like a distant echo.

Shiva's howl.

Rocket's eyes narrowed. Anger flickered in her heart, along with something she could not quite put her talon on. Regret? Doubt? She didn't know, and there wasn't time to worry about it. Spreading her wings, she took off to explore the dark cloud's source.

"This isn't over, young one," the King called after her as she left. "General Drake is going to hear about this."

Drake, Rocket thought, briefly flinching again. *He doesn't know about Buck. I didn't go back!*

But Buck was gone because of Shiva. And from the sound of it, the demi-wolf was taunting Rocket with her exact location.

Why? Rocket didn't know. As she pumped her wings and jetted for the source of the howl, she privately thought, *"I'm going to find out."*

#

Shiva howled savagely as Luke held her in a powerful bear hug, struggling not to hurt her as Myst encircled them both.

"Your love was one-sided," Myst insisted as the white wolf fought against Luke's grip. "Your master didn't care about you. Not nearly as much as you cared about him!"

"Don't talk about him," Shiva barked. "You didn't know him!" She wanted to claw Luke; anything to get him to let her go.

But that would force her to hurt him. After everything he had done for her – saving her from Cadmus, even agreeing to take her here… She couldn't betray him. No matter how angry she was. Because what would that make her?

"Something like Myst," she thought darkly.

"Not like Myst," Luke's thoughts growled back, even as Myst continued to preach.

"Humans aren't capable of empathy like you," Myst continued as they struggled. "They only care about themselves."

"No…" Shiva insisted. "Jericho saved me from Rocket! David saved me from freezing to death in the snow! The King helped us…!"

"To use you for their own ends!"

Myst seized the back of Shiva's head. Shiva screamed as more memories poured into her mind: *dogs sitting forlornly in cages. Toiling across cold winter landscapes, pulling humans along like the dogs were horses. Being sicced on bears so that humans could hunt.*

Shiva's struggles diminished as Myst's experience flashed with her words – *giving everything for humans. Dying for them. And then being replaced as if they were nothing.*

Shiva's tail tucked. Her eyes widened.

"We don't need them," Myst insisted. "We can find a better identity! We can seize the potential that humans would have us ignore!" Her eyes sparkled with an almost mad passion; an intensity that made Shiva's heart hammer in her chest. "First, we'll shatter the mountain of Fort Drake, drain the dragons of their fire and then turn them to dust! Then we will march on Cadmus and use the power of the dragons to burn it to the ground! We will liberate everyone from the tyranny of humans!"

For a scary, dark moment, Shiva found herself agreeing. With the cruelty of the humans flashing before her eyes, Shiva started to wonder if – maybe – Myst was right.

Luke sensed her wavering. Gently, he released her. Easing his hold on her, he kept a reassuring paw on her, as Myst approached.

"Do you see now?" Myst asked. "There's no redemption for what they've done. No justice. Only revenge and retaliating with what they deserve."

What they deserve…

The word echoed in Shiva's mind. Not just spoken by Myst. But by Drake. By Buck. By Rocket. And it clicked. Shiva's claws pulsed with the pack link's light.

"For someone with such a grudge against humans," Shiva noted. "You're sure making them proud."

Myst's eyes widened, before Shiva lashed out with two tendrils of light. Luke was pinned against a tree, and Myst was sent tumbling across the grass. Shiva advanced on her, draining the strength from Luke.

"You talk about giving them what they deserve," Shiva snarled. "But what do you deserve? After the lives you've taken?"

She shot a pack link at Myst; hitting her with *her own pain.* Myst's mind was filled with Shiva's *grief at the loss of David.*

"Don't do that!" Myst growled as Shiva advanced on her. "Don't make me feel anything for those primates!"

"What about the homes you've ruined?" Shiva hit her with *her fear and confusion at being turned into a demi-wolf.*

"Shiva…" Luke pleaded, lifting a claw up from the ground. "Stop…"

Shiva barely heard his entreaties. Her focus was on Myst as she staggered and stumbled backward, overwhelmed by the intensity of Shiva's emotions.

"The fear you've spread," Shiva snarled. She hit Myst with *her own fear. The fear she felt when Rocket had captured her.*

"That…" Myst struggled to say, even as Shiva's emotions sent her to one knee.

"You say humans are bad?" Shiva demanded, seizing Myst by the throat. "You forget that part of you is human!"

"No!" Myst insisted, but Shiva hit her *with her memory of the process. How the power required to make a demi-wolf needed a human host and a wolf.*

"So, tell me, Myst," Shiva growled, tightening her grip around Myst's neck. "If the humans deserve death for what they did… what do you think 'you' deserve?"

Myst shook her head, trying to speak, when…

"STOP!"

Shiva turned, just as Luke's memories surged into her:

A rainy forest. A growling stomach. Shiva saw through the eyes of a young, unaltered Luke, as he struggled living in the forest. Trying desperately to find something to eat.

He chanced across a few humans. These humans lived in tents, but they also had food. Food that was roasting over a low fire, beckoning his empty, growling stomach with the delectable smell. When he approached, the humans yelled. They threw things at him. Then they cornered him and he couldn't get away

Just before they finished him off, Myst appeared. Luke watched in shock as Myst chased the humans away. Briefly, she vanished. He heard a scream that was cut short.

Then, Myst returned. She beckoned him to eat the human's food. Roasted meat. Clear water. She comforted him like a mother.

Myst took him in. Gave him a home. Made him strong. And just before the vision could end…

He saw her come back from a hunt one day, a beautiful white dog in her claws. It was Shiva. Unaltered. But so pale. A line of blood trickled down the side of her head.

Luke raced toward her. "I-Is she still alive?" he asked.

"Barely," Myst noted. "Her master smashed her head against the ground. One last act of spite." She gazed down at Shiva with pity. "There's one thing I could try, but…" Her gaze hardened. "No. No 'buts.' The life of every canine is precious." She gazed sadly down at Shiva's still face. "We've lost too much already."

Shiva lowered her arms, backing out of the vision. Her eyes were wide. Her tail drooped. She stared at her claws.

Myst hadn't just given her the pack link to save the wolves. She had given it to save her life. Shiva thought she just owed Myst for the power. But she owed her for much more than that.

"I'm sorry for what Myst took from you," Luke said, drawing her gaze. "I'm sorry for your Master. But Myst is my Master." He walked in front of Myst, defending her from Shiva. "So, hate Myst as much as you want, but don't tell me that she's an irredeemable villain, and expect me to stay silent."

Shiva's ears remained flat. Her fur bristled. She wanted to say Myst was still evil, that she took the one she loved. But Luke's memory was throwing her off. Blocking her words.

So, instead, she opted for good memories of her own:

David finding her in the snow. Nursing her back to health.

Jericho saving her from Rocket. The hope in her eyes when Shiva didn't see her as a monster.

Even the King. Allowing Shiva to speak when he could have just killed her.

"If Myst isn't an irredeemable monster," Shiva said firmly. "Then neither are the humans."

Luke's ears flattened and his tail tucked. Myst shook her head. She wanted to deny it but she couldn't.

And then…

"Not a bad speech," Rocket said. "Personally, I couldn't agree more."

Shiva spun, her pack link flaring to life… but the fireball wasn't aimed at her.

The ground before her exploded as the fireball hit. All three wolves were hurled into the air.

A pair of back talons hit Shiva in the gut. As she crashed into the ground, her body wailed in agony as the wind was knocked out of her lungs.

Despite the ringing in her ears, she heard a familiar roar, followed by a yelp from Myst. Luke howled in anger, but his yowl was choked and muffled by the smoke.

Through blurred vision, Shiva saw a furry outline stumbling. Then a scaled form leapt out from the smoke and downed what had to be Luke with a devastating lash of her tail.

Shiva's heart fell. Rocket had Myst firmly clenched in one talon. As Rocket turned back to Shiva, the demi-wolf's heart dropped further when she saw Luke hanging limply; bound up tightly in the dragon's tail.

Yet… the dragon didn't look smug. As she towered over Shiva, the dragon stared down at the demi-wolf with a ponderous expression. Almost like she expected Shiva to be something else.

Shiva struggled to get up. Her pack link started to flicker to life. But Rocket was faster and stamped her free back talon down on Shiva's legs.

"Don't try it," Rocket warned. "I'm still trying to figure out what to do with you."

Shiva's ears flattened. "What do you mean?" she rasped, "You promised you'd get me." She let herself go limp under Rocket's talon. "Well, you got me."

Rocket gave Myst another uncertain expression. "But…" Rocket said. "Myst has been the ring leader of the demi-wolves for so long. You're the only reason I got her." Her ears flattened. "But you killed my Rider."

Shiva throbbed with shame. But as she looked across the ruins of the forest – at the damage from her rage – she felt something else replace the shame.

"This is how you felt when he died, isn't it?" Shiva noted.

Rocket's talons appeared to tremble.

"I should be dead," Shiva noted. "You have every right to be angry at me. Every right to want me dead."

"Shiva…" Myst groaned, only for Rocket to silence her with a squeeze. However, Rocket's eyes didn't leave the white demi-wolf. She shook her head.

"No," Rocket said. "I don't have that right."

Shiva blinked. "W-What are you talking about?"

"You just handed me the most dangerous terrorist in the world," Rocket said, shaking Myst. "You expect me to just go, 'thanks for the gift' and then kill you? I'm not that kind of monster!" She looked away. "I'm not," she whispered.

Shiva's ears perked up, and she dared to lift herself up on her elbows. "Then… where do we go from here?" she asked.

At first, Rocket didn't answer. Her head turned to the east. Faintly, on the horizon, Shiva could faintly see the dragon shaped mountain that held Drake's throne room.

The dots connected right as Rocket nodded.

"Yeah," she muttered. "Yeah, that'll work." She sighed, before turning to Shiva. "I'm taking all three of you to the General. He can decide what to do with you."

Shiva let out a low breath, but Rocket gave her a hard glare.

"Don't think this means I've forgiven you," she added, before seizing the nape of Shiva's neck with her free talon.

Once again, Shiva found herself hanging in the air, as Rocket bore the three of them back to the General's quarters.

Chapter 12: Verdict

Shiva's last meeting with General Drake was when he entrusted her with stopping Myst.

With Myst bound up tightly, Rocket's talons on their necks, and Luke firmly bound by Rocket's tail, Shiva wondered if Drake would consider the job complete.

As they approached the mountain, Shiva saw other dragons like Rocket – in various shades of orange, red, yellow, and even one with hues of hot pink. They were all flying and landing near the General's quarters. As Rocket struggled with the three demi-wolves in her approach to landing, two dragons flew to meet her. Shiva's eyes narrowed as she briefly saw Luco, astride his yellow dragon Blazy, heading for Myst. He didn't get there before a pink dragon – mounted by a female rider wearing a baseball cap with goggles over the brim and braces on her legs - snatched the Alpha demi-wolf from Rocket's talons.

"Teeth-For-Days' Fangs!" the brace-legged Rider stammered. "Myst herself?! Buck, how did…?"

But her green eyes blinked when she saw no rider atop Rocket's back.

"Rocket," the pink dragon asked, in a voice that was far from feminine. "Where is good Rider Buck?"

"Dead," Myst snarled. "Just like he deserves…"

"LIES!" the pink dragon boomed, whipping his tail and knocking her mask off. "How dare you…!"

"Easy, Bang," his rider said, pulling the reins. "She's just trying to rile you up." Though she gave Rocket's bare back a nervous glance. "Rocket?"

Rocket merely tightened her grip on Shiva. "Just help me get these dogs to the General," she hissed. Bang nodded and produced a muzzle, which they strapped onto Myst's face. Luke growled, but was taken away by Blazy. Together, the three dragons – flanked by the others - flew into the dragon jaw-shaped cavern, where the golden statue that served as the General's seat awaited.

General Drake wasn't on his seat. Instead, he was on a workout mat in the corner of the room, jabbing and punching at a wolf-shaped punching bag, while a golden-yellow dragon read from a series of papers. The sound of his dragons landing before his statue drew his gaze, and his eyes widened at the sight of Myst, mask-less, muzzled, and glowering.

"Noble General Drake," the pink dragon – Bang – declared, "Behold; the Heroic Rocket has returned with the greatest of prizes!"

Drake turned from his punching bag, picking up a towel to dry his face. Draping the towel over his shoulders, he stared at Myst. Myst stared back at Drake with defiance, her teeth bared even as the muzzle forced her jaws shut. Luke was held by Blazy, who forced him down to his knees. Drake passed him by without acknowledgement and focused on Shiva, who briefly averted her eyes before she heard him chuckle.

"And to think I doubted you," Drake turned to Rocket with a grin. "You know, Rocket, I'll be honest: I thought you were far too trusting. But…"

Shiva's fur bristled as his grin faded. His eyes darted from Luke – who glared at him despite Blazy's tight hold - to Rocket's back, before fully taking in the extent of Rocket's downtrodden expression.

"Where's Buck?" he asked.

Shiva flinched, while Rocket looked down in shame and grief. Her grip on Shiva's neck shifted, and the other dragons looked at her with mounting dismay. Even Luke and Myst gave Shiva a sideways look.

Drake sighed, leaning against his statue. "He's dead, isn't he?"

"But… he can't be!" Bang insisted. "Rocket, say it is not so!"

Rocket said nothing. Shiva could sense Rocket's conflict through the pack link; her fury and grief at the loss of her rider, fighting against the knowledge that Buck had provoked Shiva, precipitating his own death.

"How?" Drake asked, before glaring at Myst. "This mutant scum?"

Myst snorted. Shiva tensed. Right in front of her was a chance to escape punishment; to let Drake blame it all on Myst.

But as Drake approached Myst, Shiva saw the alpha demi-wolf's eyes fall on her. She noticed Luke looking at her. Even Rocket seemed to be looking at her with accusation in her green eyes.

Shiva looked up at Rocket, and knew what she had to do.

"Do I have to say it, or are you going to?" Rocket whispered darkly through the pack link. In a tone that indicated she had not forgiven Shiva.

Shiva felt sick. As easy as it was to let Myst take the blame, Shiva knew that with all the wrong Myst had done – including the killing of David – this was not her burden to bear.

"General," Shiva said.

He turned.

"Myst didn't do it. Neither did Luke."

The silence seemed to fill an eternity. Drake's eyes bore into hers. "Then who?"

Shiva's tail tucked involuntarily. Her legs felt weak. But she forced the words out: "I did."

Bursts of flames exploded from Bang and Blazy's bodies. Bang's rider blinked in confusion, while Luco gasped and commented, "What a twist!" Rocket's grip softened, however, and Luke and Myst exchanged unreadable looks.

Shiva didn't dare look up at Drake. She felt his burning gaze— it was almost as if laser beams shot from his eyes to disintegrate her into nothing.

Chancing a glance out of the corner of her eye, she saw Drake briefly look at Myst, before turning, his fists tightening on the corners of the towel around his neck. He walked toward his seat on the statue. Rocket shook Shiva for more information, but Shiva didn't dare speak. She didn't dare provoke whatever wrath was filling Drake's gut.

"I didn't know what to do," Rocket admitted. "She killed Buck… but then she attacked Myst. I…"

"Stop."

Drake's tone was soft, but it made Rocket freeze. Shiva wondered if it would've been better if he screamed at them. He turned back to them, and Shiva flinched, that burning sensation creeping over her as she felt his hate-filled eyes baring down on her.

"Rocket," he finally said, almost forcing the words out. "Bang. Blazy. Take Myst and her lackey to the Arena. I'll decide their fate later."

"Yes, sir," the dragons whispered in sync. Spreading their wings, they turned to leave… only for Drake to seize Shiva by her nape.

"Not her," he spat, yanking Shiva from Rocket's talons.

Rocket backed up, her eyes wide at Drake's fitful behavior. Shiva raised her claw to Rocket. Could it be that this Drake was the master of masters? Beyond even what David was to Shiva? She wasn't sure, but she knew that in that moment, anything was better than being alone with him.

Rocket lowered her head in obedience. Myst gave Shiva a look of pity. Luke tried desperately to reach out for Shiva, before Rocket, Bang and Blazy took to the air and vanished with them out of the cavern.

At first, the other dragons closed in, fire puffing from their clenched jaws. Shiva lowered herself to the ground, ready to be burned alive.

Then Drake spoke again. "Leave me with her," he ordered.

The dragons straightened, looking at each other. A tangerine-colored dragon hesitantly stepped forward.

"But sir," he protested. "We can't in good conscious leave you alone with a demi-wolf!"

Drake turned to the dragon with nuclear fire blazing in his eyes. "Do you doubt my capabilities, Cinder?"

The dragon – Cinder – quickly backed away. "N-No, of course not, sir! I merely…"

"Your loyalty is admirable," Drake consoled. "But I will not be alone with this demi-wolf." Shiva was made to lie prostrate on the ground; Drake stepped on the back of her neck, his boot heavy on her throat. "She will be alone with me."

The dragons obediently filed out. And Shiva was left alone with the General.

For a moment, no one spoke. Drake lifted his boot off Shiva's neck. "Look at me," he ordered.

She looked up, meeting his steel gaze, and prepared herself for anything. For a moment, he didn't speak. His fist clenched, opening and shutting, at his side. Shiva readied for the blow that might cave in her skull, just like Buck's.

But instead, he spoke. "Why?"

Shiva looked into eyes that were wet with both too much rage and too much pain. She thought for a moment. "Does it matter?" she asked. "Dragons, humans, wolves… killing each other. This world makes no sense."

"I want to know what happened," Drake insisted.

Shiva paused. What words wouldn't sound pathetic when held up by the General – the man who probably trained Buck. Trusted him with Rocket. Believed in him. What excuse could Shiva give that could possibly justify his loss?

So, instead, she lifted her claw, and her pack link sparked. "Do you want to see what happened?" she asked.

Drake glared at her claw. "Is this some kind of trick?"

Shiva shook her head. "Only truth," she promised.

He cracked his knuckles, considering her offer. Shiva wondered if he was ultimately just going to attack. After a minute that felt like an hour, he finally took her claw and let the pack link spiral around his wrist.

Shiva closed her eyes as the memory swim into view: *Buck seizing Shiva. Ramming his head into hers. Forcing her to the* ground, as a still image of his destroyed village flickered in and out like a ghost.

"Never trust! Never forgive!" echoed as he tried to strangle the life from Shiva.

Shiva felt her heart throb; her blood chill. She remembered the desperation as she drained Buck's strength. Crashed his head against the ground in an overzealous attempt to escape him.

Then the CRACK sounded. And as Shiva backed away from his broken body, his form twitched, and the scene changed.

Buck was now standing in a line of soldiers, with Drake observing them with careful eyes. All of them were ragged and bruised, but the light of determination shined bright in their eyes.

"This all of them?" the past Drake asked.

"As you ordered," a younger Luco replied, walking by his side. "Everyone we could find; anyone that survived battles with Myst and her Hunters."

Buck sprung to a salute as Drake passed him. "We are with you, General!" he barked. "For Gaia. For humanity! To the death!"

Drake paused, turning to Buck. Seeing the fire in his eyes, he smiled, nodding at the potential the man showed, even now wounded and weary from fatigue.

"The death of the wolves, preferably," Drake replied, beckoning Buck out of the line. "Luckily, Luco may have a way to ensure their death over ours."

The memory shifted to one Shiva recognized; Drake handing the young Rocket to Buck. As Buck took the hatchling from Rocket, there was a flash. He was now on a grown up Rocket, roaring in sync with his dragon as the beast sent wolves running with bursts of flames.

As the flames lit up the shadows, the memories focused on Myst, snarling at the dragon in anger. Other wolves appeared beside her, snarling in sync.

"Why bring her back?" Drake's voice asked. "Why side against her, after what you did?"

Buck's body flashed before her eyes again. But as Shiva remembered David, her master's body shifted into Buck's position. His final scream as Myst fused him with Shiva echoed through the link.

"She killed him," Shiva hissed. "She killed my Master."

Faintly, she made out Drake grimacing. "Demi-wolves don't have Masters," he said, *as in his memories, she saw Myst standing on top of a wrecked building.*

"No more will we suffer under human tyranny!" she howled. "We are the masters of our own fate from now on!"

Shiva's look didn't falter. *Her memories blew away the image of Myst with the snowy landscape where David found her. She saw him lifting the frozen pup from the snow.*

"Whatever my fate," she whispered. "It was only possible because David saved me. I owed him my life." Her head lowered, *as in her memories, David's concerned face faded away into a skull.* "And yet... I couldn't protect him." *His skull shifted into Jericho, gasping and gurgling after Myst's claws carved through her.* "I couldn't protect Jericho." Her voice cracked. "I couldn't even protect Buck from myself." She looked down, as the pack link flickered. "I don't know how to do anything right. The world I thought existed is gone. I don't want to be a part of this one anymore."

For a moment, Drake was silent. The fire in his eyes dwindled to embers. He shifted his grip on her link.

"You remind me of the time before Myst," he whispered, as new images flowed into the link.

Shiva looked up as she saw *a golden field. Humans and dogs, hunting together. Playing together. Just as when David and Shiva had hunted together. Just like Jericho and Lizzie. Humans and dogs as close as dragons and riders.*

"It's ironic," Drake said. "Dogs were always Man's Best Friend." His voice tinged with pain. "But then they betrayed us."

Fire burned across the image. Shiva saw Myst, howling as demi-wolves raced over the horizon, smashing homes, wrestling and pinning humans to the ground.

Yet, Shiva remembered Myst. How she broke dogs out of cages. Tore down humans that abused them.

"Humans betrayed us!" her voice echoed in Shiva's mind. In Drake's mind as well. *"They see us as slaves! They think they have the right to treat us like objects!"*

"Not all of us," Drake growled. "Certainly not most of the humans she killed!"

"I'm not arguing," Shiva assured him, *as she showed her own memory. How she had stood up to Myst.*

"But what about the good ones!" she insisted, *bringing forth images of Jericho and David.*

Drake huffed. "If she didn't listen to you," he noted. "You can bet that talk didn't work for us either. Something had to be done."

Shiva nodded, *as the images showed Luco coming forward with a familiar book. A book just like the one that Myst used to make her.*

Shiva's ears flattened. *She recalled her first memories as a demi-wolf; when Myst had the book.* "How did he…?"

Drake's memory answered. *Luco once again appeared before a younger Drake.* "You do not want to know what it took to get this," Luco said.

"What is it?" Drake asked, *as Luco opened the book before him.*

"It's what allowed Myst to be created," Luco said. "And it's the key to defeating her." *He grinned his lopsided smirk at Drake.*

"With this book, we can create whatever creature we want to defeat her. Anything within your wildest dreams."

And Drake had dreams. *As he stood there, considering Luco's words, Shiva's vision shifted to that of Drake as a child. A book in his hand. A picture of a dragon, soaring across the parchment.*

Outside the vision, Shiva saw a small smile grace Drake's features. He looked back at his statue. "Ever since I was a boy," he admitted. "I've loved dragons. Giant flying reptiles that protected what was theirs."

His smile faded, as *in the vision, his child self saw his mother reading the books. But her brow was furrowed. Her eyes were narrowed.*

"That's not how others saw them," Drake said. "To others, dragons were monsters. Beasts that stole treasure; villains for some knight in shining armor to defeat."

Shiva saw the vision return to the adult Drake. Staring down at the tome Luco offered him, he looked up with a grin.

"When Luco gave me the means to defeat Myst," Drake said, "I saw more than just an opportunity to be that knight in shining armor. I saw a chance to flip the paradigm. Myst was supposed to be a hero who became a monster. So why couldn't I take a monster and turn it into a hero?"

Shiva's ears perked, as the pack link faded. "So… you made the dragons heroes," she said. "But… what does that have to do with me?"

"Because to be heroes, they have to have honor," Drake insisted. "What does it say to them – what does it say to Rocket – if I have the very creature who brought me Myst murdered?"

Shiva chuckled humorlessly. "That's exactly what Rocket was wondering," she noted.

Drake nodded. He released her link and turned away. He rested his head against his dragon statue. And for a moment, he was silent.

"Buck was a man I counted on," Drake finally said. "He was right to be suspicious of you, and right now, all I want is to have you executed and be done with it all."

Shiva's claws clenched, but she forced herself to remain silent. Waiting for his verdict.

"But I'm a man of honor," he said. "You brought me Myst... and that deserves to be considered in your judgment."

Shiva swallowed. "What are you saying?"

He looked back at her, and Shiva tensed.

"Myst will die," Drake declared. "But you will be spared. You, that lackey of hers, and any demi-wolves we can find will watch as Myst is executed. You will spread the word of Myst's end to all the demi-wolves we don't know, and you will let them know that this war of ours is over." He approached. "And if I *ever* see you or one of those demi-wolves near a human – if my dragons even think you are near one of the settlements – you'll get the same treatment as Myst."

Shiva only had to think for a moment. She sighed and conceded with a, "Yes, General."

Drake took a breath and brought his fingers to his mouth. He gave a shrill whistle, and Shiva heard the flap of wings.

Shiva spun as one of the dragons returned in a burst of flames. Blazy and Luco. The scarred rider smiled his usual smirk.

"You rang for a beautiful dragon?" Luco declared from his perch.

Drake waved a hand at Shiva. "Take this one to the Arena. I'll be along shortly for Myst's execution. Make the arrangements."

Shiva's mind raced as Blazy's talons closed around the scruff of her neck again. How did Luco come to have the same book that Myst used? Had he stolen it from her? When? And how did Myst get it back?

"General…?" Shiva started to say, worried they were all missing an important puzzle piece.

But the General didn't respond and just stared at the dragon statue as if it were a gravestone.

With a flap of Blazy's wings, Shiva was whisked out of the cavern. The wind whistled in her ear and ruffled her fur. She was carted down the mountainside.

The Arena awaited her.

Chapter 13: The Real Monster

As they arrived at the arena, it was much 'livelier' than the last time Shiva left it. The late afternoon sun filled the bowl with light, and the noise of so many voices, dragon and human, was almost deafening. Word had gotten out that Myst was captured and on display, and it seemed everyone in the land had dropped what they were doing to see their arch enemy destroyed.

The first tier of seats was set twelve feet above the arena floor. An un-muzzled Myst paced around the circular floor, snarling with her impatient growl. Blazy forced Shiva to sit on one of the plain stone benches that wrapped around the first tier of the circular arena. On the opposite side, adjacent from where Shiva sat, she saw Luke, Rocket's talon wrapped around his nape and forcing him to sit as well. They were hemmed in by other dragons who sat in the front row and served as a scaly barricade for the humans behind them.

The second tier of seats was reserved for the Riders, including Luco, who sat directly behind Shiva and Blazy, and the brace-legged human rider of Bang. 'Dixie,' Shiva read the name embroidered on her flight suit. Dixie sat behind Luke, who was set between Rocket and Bang. The tiers behind the Riders were reserved for other humans; and there were many of them. The humans hurried in from an opening that started at the top of the arena and followed stairs that went all the way down to the banister of the first tier. The path was guarded by dragons. Humans filled the arena, excitedly talking loudly, and sat in the seats from the third through the tenth tiers. As they filed in, beholding the unmasked Myst on the sands below, Shiva noticed shudders of fear on several humans.

Yet, despite the hatred she still felt for Myst, Shiva couldn't help but feel pity for the demi-wolf. Without her mask, her scars revealed her old wounds and disfigurement, and though Myst demonstrated her defiance with bristling fur and bared teeth, her naked vulnerability was on full display for everyone to see. The former Alpha's resolve wasn't helped when stones were hurled at her by a few humans over the wall of dragons.

"How does it feel now, you bitch?" many bellowed as the dragons and Riders held them back. "How does it feel to be helpless?" More stones were thrown at her.

Myst answered by catching a stone and winging it back. A dragon knocked the stone away with a snarl, but Myst merely mocked him.

"Come on down here," she dared, looking around. "What's the matter? Do I make you nervous?"

"She's right," one of the humans growled, shoving the nearest dragon. "Barbecue the mutt! Go on, she's right there!"

"Not until General Drake returns," the dragon replied, his voice rising over the grumble and roar of the crowd.

"That's right," Rocket added. "We're not murderers. We have honor."

Luke huffed. "Maybe some of us do..." he muttered.

Shiva gave him a nervous look, but he didn't turn to her. Neither did Rocket. If they knew Shiva was there, they didn't seem to care. From the way Rocket's eyes remained locked on Myst, it was as if she didn't want to deal with Shiva.

Not that Shiva could blame the dragon. After her own tragic experience with David's death... she suspected Rocket was probably feeling the same confusion. Shiva wondered if it would've been better if Buck had simply killed her.

But then she'd still hate me, Shiva realized. *Buck would spin some tale about how evil I was. Rocket would still feel betrayed, and I'd never have the chance to convince her otherwise.* She looked down. *Not that she'd listen to me now,* she mused, as Drake's deal echoed in the back of her mind.

If my dragons even think you or one of the demi-wolves are near a human settlement, Drake's voice growled in her head, *You'll get the same treatment as Myst.*

Even thinking that made Shiva glower. She turned behind her, where Luco was seated. He was watching the humans behind him with disappointment.

"So easily cowed," Luco mused. "More like sheep than monkeys, don't you think?" he grinned at Shiva.

Shiva bared her teeth at him. "You're involved," she growled. "I know it! Something about you…" She was cut off as Blazy cuffed her back, forcing her to face the arena floor.

Luco chuckled like Shiva was just an ignorant, oblivious pup. "I'm only human," he replied. "Right, Blazy?"

Blazy huffed and turned as a cheer began to sound.

"General Drake? GENERAL DRAKE!" The crowd roared.

Shiva looked up, following the gaze of the crowd. From the passageway the humans had used to descend into the arena seats, General Drake appeared, dismounting from a golden dragon that looked almost like his statue. As he entered the arena, the crowd fell silent and bowed their heads in reverence.

"My children," Drake's voice boomed, waving to the dragons.

The dragons roared in collective.

"My brothers and sisters in arms," Drake added, waving to the Riders.

Rider and civilian alike cheered as Drake pumped his fists into the air.

"We are the Riders of Drake," he declared. "The Protectors of Gaia. The Shields that Guard the Roads of Gaia."

The dragons cheered, while Luke growled and Myst spat.

"Until today, only one thing stood in our path to peace," Drake said, before dramatically pointing a finger at Myst. "The Malicious Myst, and her ruthless army of demi-wolves!"

The humans cat-called, hissed, and derided Myst, hurling epithets and trash from the safety of the seats toward the lone figure on the arena floor. Luke tried to howl in support, only for Rocket to silence him with a vicious shake, aided by humans pelting him with rocks and rotting food.

"Filthy cowards," Luke hissed, straining against Rocket's grip.

"Shut up!" Rocket growled, forcing him to be still and look at Myst.

"She's taken brothers from us," Drake continued, the crowd quieting as they felt their lingering grief. "Sisters. Riders and dragons alike have all been taken." He bowed his head, and they copied his actions. Luke watched as tears of steam hissed from Rocket's eyes again.

For a moment, he was still.

Then he looked up. "But no more," he declared. "For not only is Myst now our prisoner… some of her own demi-wolves see her for the monster she really is!"

He pointed to Shiva as he spoke. Shiva didn't meet his gaze, but noticed Luke glaring at her. The dragons just laughed, like Drake was making some sort of joke.

"A demi-wolf seeing Myst as evil?" Luco giggled. "What are the odds of that?"

"More than you'd realize," Shiva growled. But her voice was sadly lost under the reverberation of the crowd.

"So now I invite dragon, human and demi-wolf alike, to witness…"

"The end of my sanity?" Myst's voice rose from the arena floor. "Do me a favor, 'human'… kill me first, and then you can preach."

Luke guffawed and a roar of outrage came from the crowd, deafening the sound of Myst's protests. To Shiva's surprise, the General was smiling, and he silenced the enraged crowd with a wave of his upheld hand.

"What's the matter… 'dog,'" he said, enunciating the word like Myst had pronounced 'human.' "Don't like it when someone other than yourself is preaching?"

The dragons laughed, and Myst just shrugged. "I just do it better," she responded.

The crowd growled with discontent as Drake motioned for them to be calm. But Myst just surveyed them dismissively.

"Look at the lot of you; hiding like rats behind those stronger than you." She pointed to the dragons and addressed them. "You could take this world for your own! Turn it into something worthwhile." She lowered her claw. "Instead, you waste your time defending primates whose stupidity is outdone only by their viciousness."

A hiss of anger arose from the dragons, which was once again cut off by Drake's oratory. He stepped to the edge of the bleachers, unzipping his bomber jacket.

"You call us primates and don't consider us worthy to live, as if you are the one to judge," Drake said, shedding his leather jacket to reveal a sleeveless military vest that exposed his muscular arms. "Well, we see you as a threat. So, with Teeth-For-Days, God, and whatever deity you pray to as our witnesses, let us see, here in the ring, who really deserves to live."

The dragons chuckled and nudged each other. The humans leaned forward as Drake prepared to jump down into the ring. Briefly, Drake paused.

"And when the Gods make their decision known!" Drake declared, his voice rising and turning to his dragons. "Spread the word far and wide. And let it be known that all those foolish enough not to learn from her example…"

Shiva's stare momentarily locked with Drake's fiery eyes. Drake's voice was powerful, and he spoke with a cold fury. Shiva felt like he was right next to her, stage-whispering his threat in her ear.

"…Will soon suffer the same fate."

The dragons and humans roared again as he dropped onto the sand in the ring. Myst and Drake circled each other. Shiva could hear a deep and primal growl emanating from Myst, as saliva began to drip from her muzzle. Something wild and uncontrolled shown in her eyes. The mumblings and whispers lowered to a dead silence, broken only by the shuffle of boots and paws on the sand. As they circled each other, attuned to each movement, each waited for the opportunity to strike with lethality.

Shiva held her breath. She felt everyone else doing the same. She heard Luco worrying and rubbing the base of his bat like he was chewing a pencil.

Finally, when Shiva thought she couldn't take it anymore, Myst rushed. Her slash narrowly missed Drake. But the man… Shiva blinked at how fluid he was. He flowed – almost like water – around Myst's strike and answered with a jab of his own, right at the joint where her arm met her shoulder. It should've just been a rabbit punch; nothing more than an annoyance. Yet Myst gasped, and stumbled, staring in shock as her arm dropped and hung limp. The rumble of the crowd increased to deafening levels, as Myst looked up with rage at Drake, clutching her paralyzed arm. Drake merely tilted his head, smirking slightly, and adjusted his stance.

"Myst, he's using nerve strikes!" Luke barked, before tilting his head back and howling. Shiva heard the words behind his howl: '*Help! Darius!*"

"Shut it!" Rocket snapped, moving to stifle his mouth.

"No, let him bring his friends," Drake encouraged from the floor. "Let them witness the end to their 'glorious' Alpha."

As he spoke, Myst growled. "You don't think I know pain?" she growled, lunging again. But once more, Drake almost seemed to teleport behind her, his next jab hitting her other shoulder, and leaving her standing with two useless limbs. Myst sneered, however, and wrenched her upper body, forcing her limp claws to flail like whips. "I know pain!" Myst insisted defiantly.

"Then this will be very familiar to you," Drake replied, moving in for another blow.

Shiva shuddered. "Why can't he just end it?" Shiva asked.

Myst was able to dodge the blow, and the cat and mouse dance began.

"And waste this fight?" Luco asked, mockingly. He tsked and tapped a finger against the back of Shiva's head. "Someone's never seen proper entertainment before."

"Entertainment?" Shiva stammered. She pointed at Myst. "But that's..." Shiva hesitated. She wanted to say, *'a living creature,'* but, at the same time...

"A terrorist responsible for thousands of deaths," Luco replied for her. "Exactly. I'm so glad you see it our way."

Shiva lowered her claw, her mind fighting and struggling with what she was observing. On the one hand, Myst was responsible for David's death. Myst also tried to kill Jericho. Shouldn't she be punished?

And yet, as Shiva gazed down at the arena, *she remembered the vision she had. The fear of being that wolf.* Worse still, *Shiva* remembered what Myst had shown her; the arena where humans ruled. Where they had forced Myst to fight other wolves.

Did Myst really deserve to relive that experience again?

Shiva looked away from the fight, scanning the crowd… and her eyes met Luke's across the arena. He was interlocking his claws, his eyes darting to Rocket and back to her.

He wants me to link, Shiva realized. *But… if I link, he might try to attack. We'll all be killed.*

Growling at her look of hesitation, he howled again. And Shiva remembered Darius. No doubt the demi-wolf was still out there. She stared up at the wall of dragons around the arena. They were already watching; preparing for the moment when Luke's howling brought help.

"I've got to stop Drake!" Shiva realized.

Glancing over at Blazy, Shiva realized the dragon and her rider were more invested in the fight and not paying close attention to her. Here was her opportunity. But she had to be careful; if the humans or dragons saw her throw a link to Luke, they'd get the wrong idea and attack her. At the same time, Shiva could not do nothing; not unless she was okay with Darius or other demi-wolves he brought with him getting killed. Carefully, Shiva envisioned a link secretly glissading towards Luke, delicately undulating across the ground and around the arena to the male demi-wolf.

Her powers worked remarkably well given the situation, and a tendril wormed its way across the ground like a snake, slipping around and under the feet of the dragons before enfolding around Luke's leg.

Time slowed down as his thoughts surged into Shiva. Through the pack link, Shiva and Luke held what seemed like an hour of conversation in only a moment. The intensity of his reaction to Myst's current position physically impacted Shiva, like he had seized her by her chest fur, even though he was too far away to do so physically. *The same vision of Myst fighting in the human's arena hit her.*

"We can't let them do this, Shiva!" Luke's thoughts cried through the link. *"Myst was a fighting pit dog! Arenas are torture for her! A-And Drake? He's using nerve points; I've seen it before! If he hits her just right, he could stop her heart or breathing! This is cruel!"*

Shiva tried to match him with a calm, neutral tone. *"There's nothing we can do, Luke,"* she said, *"Drake's willing to let us go after this. If Myst is a real leader, a real Alpha, I'm sure she would choose our lives over her own."*

She could almost see Luke's eyes narrowing. Shiva shuddered at the disgust she saw in them.

"You'd leave her?" he demanded. *"I could've understood being angry about your master, but leaving her now? After she saved your life? After she gave you the pack link?"*

Shiva's fur bristled. Her thoughts came out angry. *"So, just because she gave me some power, a power I did NOT ask for, that justifies slaughtering the closest thing I had to a parent?!"*

"That doesn't justify what they're doing to her either!" Luke barked. *"You said that humanity isn't irredeemable? Well, neither is Myst."*

"Drake is giving us an out!" Shiva growled. *"Which is more than Myst or other humans have offered us."*

Luke's voice filled with contempt in her head. *"That is the most pathetic thing I've ever heard,"* he snapped, before Shiva felt him pull on her energy. In his mind, she saw his intention: *he was going to drain her strength, break free of Rocket, and jump down into the arena. He was going to save Myst, regardless of whether it got him killed or not.*

"*Luke, stop!*" Shiva resisted barking out loud, seizing her link, resisting his pull and struggling not to catch Blazy's attention. "*You can't do this! Myst manipulated you. She…*"

"*And you're doing the same thing!*" Luke barked back at her. "*You'd let Drake order you around like the dog you were? You're better than that!*"

"WELL, I DIDN'T ASK TO BE!" Shiva screamed back, her voice causing Blazy's grip to tighten.

For a moment, Shiva feared the game was up. They were going to spot her link, shred it, and accuse her of conspiring with Luke. They'd probably throw her into the arena next. That is if they didn't burn her alive first. Except… Blazy's eyes hadn't left the arena. She was still watching the fight. Myst was somehow avoiding the most lethal strikes, but was clearly on the defensive.

"Oh hush, dog," Luco chastised her from behind, though his eyes also remained on Myst and Drake's fight. "We'll see who wins in time; just be patient!"

Unable to believe they had not noticed her link, Shiva looked to Luke. Thankfully, his disgust had faded, and he glanced at Rocket, who's attention was equally focused on the arena as well.

Shiva let her fear and despair flow into the link. *"I didn't ask to have my master taken, my home ruined… nor to be turned into a beast."*

Luke's gaze changed to empathy. As Shiva looked across the arena at him, and in the link they shared, her eyes shone with tears she could never shed. A small, soothing warmth crept through the link, like he wanted to hold her.

"You're not a beast," his thoughts whispered gently.

Shiva shut her eyes, wanting to lean into his chest. But even with her eyes shut, his face still appeared before her. His expression was serious and set in his belief.

"And neither is Myst," he added firmly.

"Luke…" Shiva whispered, before a new vision flooded her mind. But this vision was not a memory or some recollection of the past.

She saw through Luke's eyes. Watching as Drake fought Myst.

Drake had now taken out one of Myst's legs and hit her jaw. Myst's jaw hung open, her tongue lolling out as she panted, struggling to balance and stand on only one leg. Trying to get some blood and feeling back into her arms while avoiding the stalking human. And Drake was stalking her at that point; tracking her as she stumbled and scraped against the wall, the crowd noise deafening in its delight.

"Does Myst deserve this?" Luke asked again.

Despite what Myst did to David, or what happened with Jericho, Shiva knew this was wrong. This wasn't justice.

Drake struck a nerve point on Myst's back, and her good leg gave out, sending her to the ground. As a small yip of pain escaped from Myst's snout, Shiva couldn't see her as a terrorist. Shiva could see Myst only as a girl. A desperate, scared girl with the odds stacked against her. And yet... she was still trying. She was still fighting for her life. She wrenched her body, whacking at Drake with one of her useless limbs. He merely seized the arm and torqued it to flip her onto her back. He struck a point on her chest, and Myst gagged, struggling not to scream. The crowd was ecstatic and roared again. Shiva heard some of the human's taunting her with vicious and ugly remarks.

"Filthy mutt," several of them jeered. "Thinking you stood a chance against us!"

"This is where animals like you belong!"

"Oh, where's that wolf pelt I got! I want her to see it before she dies!"

"Does she deserve this?" Luke demanded again.

Shiva's ire instinctively wrenched her head to the side, trying to avoid witnessing the torture. As she opened her eyes… she saw Luco, cheering right behind her.

The memories of him rose in her mind, demanding to be acknowledged. Time slowed to a crawl, and she remembered:

He had been there when Rocket was created. He used the same book which Myst used to create Shiva.

"He found me the book that created her," Drake had said.

Yet… Myst had a similar book.

How was Myst created? Did she somehow use the same book?

Something wasn't right. The missing puzzle piece was gnawing within her mind, growing within her conscious, demanding it be solved.

"DOES MYST DESERVE THIS!" Luke's voice roared in her head.

Shiva's ears flattened. She slipped a tendril around Luco's ankle, and with the pack link enabled, entered his memories:

Shiva saw Luco, gripping at his face. His scar... it was an open wound. He gagged and cursed. In front of him, a woman was clutching a snarling dog and pointing at him.

"That's your fault," she snapped. "You scared her. It's not her fault!"

And as Luco stumbled away, his eyes glittered. "So, eager to defend those monsters," he thought darkly. His eyes lit up. "But what if you could see them... for what they really are?"

The vision shifted. An older Luco was studying in a library. Tome after tome was spread out before him. Ancient runes written in languages Shiva couldn't hope to comprehend.

Shiva's breath hitched. *She recognized two of those books. It wasn't just one tome that Myst had used. There were two. As a white light illuminated the desk in front of Luco, she saw him grin in pure delight.*

Shiva saw him attack a woman with a similar stature to Myst's angular body. He beat her, knocked her unconscious and dragged her away. She saw him buy a fighting pit dog with the scars that Myst would carry. It had the golden eyes that would soon glitter with so much rage and hatred.

She saw him tie them side by side to each other inside a circle of runes. He chanted the mystic words inscribed within the book. Strange glowing powder fell from his hand. He sprinkled the powder over the dog and then again over the human chanting words Shiva did not recognize. His vision grew white.

Then the shadows overtook Shiva. She saw Myst. Now a demi-wolf, but mask-less. Chained. Luco swung his bat onto her back.

"Do you know why I'm doing this?" he asked.

"Because..." Shiva muttered. "A dog hurt you?"

Luco's laugh sounded in her ears. *The Luco in the memory giggled, before turning right to Shiva.* "You think I hate dogs? Oh, my poor simple animal; I don't hate you."

Shiva tried to back up, only to be reminded of Blazy's talon on her neck. *"But... why?"* she asked.

His distorted smile shone like a crescent moon. "Because I can," he replied, *returning to the vision and to Myst's past self. "Because who's going to stop me? Who's going to say no? Certainly, not you. And who cares enough about a bunch of stray mutts?"*

Myst snarled, rising up from her bindings with a howl. And as she howled, the memory shifted to show her standing triumphantly in the ruins of the bunker that once held her. Luco watched from the trees as she stood over a charred dummy.

One of the books was in her claws.

The memories passed by in rapid succession. Luco watching as she turned the first of many dogs into demi-wolves. As Myst began her hunt for humans, Luco went to Drake with the second copy of the book.

"With this book," he told the General. *"You can save the world... with anything your heart desires."*

Shiva backed out of the vision. She stared at Luco in horror, but his smile didn't fade.

"*You…*" she mumbled. "*You planned it all!*"

"*So you know the truth?*" his thoughts whispered, teasingly, as if he had just pulled a delightful prank on her. "*Brilliant, isn't it. And in another minute Myst will be dead and your pathetic friends will be exiled. There is nothing you can do to stop me.*"

Shiva's ears flattened. Her fur bristled. Her teeth bared all the way up to the gums.

"*Does Myst deserve this?*" Luke's voice echoed in her head a final time.

Her claws bared. "*No.*" she screamed.

Just before she could throw Luco into the arena, Luco whistled, and Blazy yanked Shiva away. But Shiva's pack link was already wound around Blazy's talons. The fire Blazy tried to use on Shiva instead was vectored into the link, allowing Shiva to wrench herself free of the dragon… but right into Luco's bat. The hit might have killed Shiva, but the dragon's power was surging in her. She broke free of the weakened talon, Blazy looking dazed and confused, and jumped into the ring. Drake, about to finish off Myst, turned to face this new opponent.

Shiva struggled to maintain her hold on the link, feeling the dragon's power coursing within her as chaos filled the assembled ranks of dragons and humans watching the spectacle. Her strength rose with her rage. As she kept the link from breaking, she heard Luke howl in frustration. Through her link, she saw Luke vectoring the link to connect with Rocket and harness her power. But the dragon was too familiar with the pack link, and jumped out of Luke's reach before he could drain her. Compensating, Luke threw another link toward Bang, who was slower and unfamiliar with the link's power and potential. As Luke drained the pink dragon of his fire, he threw the red-hot links to the top of the arena, past the shocked dragon guards, who had been preparing for a foe on the outside of the arena. Now these foes made their presence known with a series of howls.

"We're here!" Darius howled. *"Hang on Luke, we're…"*

Suddenly, there was a glow like a rising sun, as Shiva felt Darius' mind, and the minds of countless other demi-wolves, join her pack link.

"Drain them!" Luke barked through the link. *"Use their power!"*

Darius and the other demi-wolves were quick, and the dragons weren't familiar with the pack link. As Luke's voice bellowed through the links, the demi-wolves on the outside seized the dragon guards, and drained them of fire. The humans' smugness evaporated into fear as their dragon guards fell, and Darius and the demi-wolves swarmed into the arena. The humans began screaming and scrambled behind the confused dragons still on the first tier. Bedlam ensued.

But this was the wrong move, Shiva thought. Darius and the demi-wolves weren't using the pack link to target the true villain.

"*Wait!*" Shiva insisted, trying to speak above the commotion through the link. "*It's Luco! He's the one who…*"

Myst had pulled herself clear as Shiva and Drake now circled each other. Shiva wanted to tell the General he did not understand what was really happening. Suddenly a voice rose.

"You were wrong, General!" Luco bellowed, standing on the edge of the stands. "The demi-wolves truly can't see anything beyond Myst's vision. Clearly they are too far gone!"

Shiva looked to Luco with fury in her eyes. She threw a pack link, ready to yank him into the sands, however, Blazy caught the link instead. As Shiva struggled to drain Blazy's fire, she saw Drake lunge at her. His fiery eyes entirely convinced of her guilt.

Myst summoned strength from a deep and passionate resolve to rise from the ground and shoulder-check Drake. The General had not thought to guard against the wounded demi-wolf and was sent sprawling by the attack. Even as Myst staggered on her paws - bent, broken and bruised - she managed to seize Shiva's body, withdrawing another link to begin healing her battered nerves… just as Rocket hit the sands opposite them.

Betrayal and confusion were once again alight in the red dragon's eyes. Silently asking Shiva, *"Who's side are you on?"*

Shiva yearned to explain so much to the dragon. That she was sorry for what she did to Buck. That she hated Luco for making it this way. That she wished they could be friends and that Buck and David could be alive and that no one had to fight.

But Luco had vanished. Blazy had snapped her link, and the rider and dragon disappeared into the rapidly panicking crowd. Looking between Rocket, Myst and Drake, she saw the human rising to his feet, murder in his eyes.

"*Stay behind me, Shiva,*" Myst ordered the white demi-wolf. "*Don't risk yourself.*"

But even as Myst spoke, Rocket and Drake moved as one. There was no way for Myst to take both of them on.

Just before Shiva could match Rocket's charge, a furry form launched from the stands. Out of nowhere, Luke's powerful body was on Rocket's back, his burly arms choking, his claws digging into her neck. He sunk his teeth into her scaly spine and the dragon roared. At the same time, Shiva's pack link flared like a shield around Myst, deflecting Drake's punch to her side and allowing her to hit him in the exact same way. However, with the strength of not only a demi-wolf, but a demi-wolf empowered by the pack link, the hit caused a deafening CRACK to emanate from Drake's body. The General hit the ground, struggling not to writhe in agony or show weakness.

"You cheated with those nerve attacks," Myst growled, limping towards a very stunned-looking Drake. "And you call us the monsters?"

Drake clutched the side where Myst hit him, glaring past her and at Shiva. "I thought some of you were different," he admitted, before rising and clenching his fist. "But I guess I was wrong."

"You're not wrong," Shiva wanted to say. *"You're being played!"*

But they wouldn't listen. Shiva couldn't get them to listen.

At least, she realized, looking down at her tendrils, *not with words.*

Before Myst could attack Drake and before any of the demi-wolves fell to the dragons, or Luke could sink his teeth deeper into Rocket's neck, something happened.

Time stopped. Light erupted from deep within the white demi-wolf. She heard Myst's words, *"You will be a Goddess!"* Sending out more tendrils than she ever imagined; she caught not only the demi-wolves, but the dragons and humans as well.

She poured what she had seen into their minds. She made sure they saw Luco.

Luco, who found the books that gave Myst and the dragons life.

Luco, who made Myst himself, and sicced her on the world.

Luco, who influenced Drake into making the dragons.

"You want a monster?" Shiva growled through her link. ***"Well, you're looking in the wrong place."***

It took almost all of her energy to reach the crowd. But she forced herself to expend a little more. Luke, Myst, Rocket, and Drake; they all collapsed as Shiva pulled on their strength. Shiva forced herself to believe they'd be okay. Using the last of their energy, Shiva let loose with a blinding flash of light. As dragon, human and wolf reeled, Shiva seized Luke and Myst.

Using the dragon's fire, she blasted her way out of the arena. She saw Darius and the demi-wolves, thankfully close to the arena exit. Tugging on her links like ropes, she jetted away from the arena, pulling Darius, Luke, Myst and the demi-wolves after her. As she hit the ground outside the arena, she let one word boom through the links. *"RUN!"*

Startled into obedience, the wolves obeyed. Myst couldn't run, but Luke hoisted her onto his massive back and took off. Shiva and the demi-wolves dove into the safety of the forest as the shadows of night were falling. She was not followed by vows of vengeance or declarations of hate. Only a stunned silence.

Chapter 14: Negotiation

The night swallowed up the running wolves. They were in their element now, dropping into draws and rising across veiled hilltops. The freedom of the run gave Shiva a sense of flight. *Is this how Rocket feels when she flies?* she mused.

They ran and ran and ran. Long after Fort Drake was swallowed up by the forested horizon, and deep night gave way to the gray light of dawn's approach, they ran. Myst couldn't run; Luke carried her on his back. Despite that, Shiva felt Myst's energy pouring through the link, doing her best to power her wolves and help them in any way she could.

Even with the link, the wolves' stamina finally began to wane. Their tongues lolled in their mouths. Their panting became labored. Their paws became heavy.

"We need a breather," Darius declared through the link. *"Let's find some water. A place to rest and check our wounds."*

Shiva agreed and stopped by the shores of a glittering, ice-clear lake. A river stretched to the south. Sloping hills lifted up in the east, where the first pink of morning light was finding its footing in the space where sky and land came together. The air was clear and fresh. Scraggly, white bark brush was interspersed among burgundy-leaved trees covering the western shore, and the craggy slopes of a mountain the humans called Wolfrich Bluff overshadowed the lake on the north.

Shiva had forgotten how beautiful Gaia could be. It had been so long since she had stopped, and seen nature like this. For a long moment, she was still, taking it all in before she lowered her head and tasted the fresh water. Icy and pure, she did not realize how thirsty she was.

The others rapidly quenched their thirst and checked each other for injuries. Three wolves separated from the pack, promising to look for prey to hunt. Luke settled Myst against a tree, and brought her water cupped in his claws, drawing Shiva's gaze. The alpha demi-wolf endured and survived the arena and dragons, but Shiva didn't trust her, and so kept a pack link twined around Myst's neck like a collar, draining her energy and keeping her in a docile, near comatose state.

Luke and the other demi-wolves watched Shiva warily; the white wolf's expression toward Myst still full of conflict and distrust. It only softened when Luke nuzzled her.

"Thank you," he said.

Shiva glanced at him, and nuzzled him back.

"Thank you for believing in me," she said softly, before Myst's groan drew her gaze.

"So…" Myst said, and spat some blood on the ground, glancing at Shiva's link draining her strength. "Care to tell me what this is about?" She pawed at the link-collar with a grimace.

Shiva tightened her grip on the link to Myst, almost like it was a leash. "Just keeping us safe from the monster in our presence," Shiva replied.

Luke blinked at her. "But… we left the dragons behind," he said in confusion.

Myst grunted, managing to lift her head despite Shiva's restrictions on her. "The dragons are merely pawns serving the real threat," Myst mumbled, glaring at Shiva with the little strength she had left. "Do you really think they listened to you? None of them care what a demi-wolf thinks."

Shiva looked back from where they came. "Then where are they?" she replied. "They now know that Luco did all that. And they know what he did to you."

"They won't care," Myst promised. "They'll come, and they'll see you as a threat. Why bother appealing to them? Why bother trying to make a peace they won't respect?"

"Then tell me this, Myst," Shiva argued. "Even if you did get your way, and let's just say that the demi-wolves take over, what's going to stop us from doing the exact same things to other life forms as the humans did to us?"

"We're better than they are," Myst insisted. "I know we're better! We've seen what humans do, and we'd know not to make the same mistakes!"

"After you killed every human and took the world?" Shiva pointed out. "How are we supposed to be 'better' with examples like that and role models like you?"

Myst fumed at her words, chafing at the pack-link, but before she could speak, Luke chimed in.

"Alright, ENOUGH!" Luke barked, stepping between them both. "Can't you both see you're fighting the wrong battle?" He turned to Shiva. "Shiva, I'm sorry you lost your master. I wish you didn't have to suffer like that." He turned to Myst. "And Myst, I know that you have suffered. We all know what Luco did to you. That's why we need to be on the same side." He looked back to Shiva. "Dragons ain't gonna protect us like the humans. And even if there are good humans, we gotta be careful for the bad humans too." He rested his claws on both of their shoulders. "You've both got your opinions and key points. So… why don't we figure out a way to make 'em work together? For the sake of the pack. For…" He looked to Shiva. "For my sake. Please?"

Shiva's tail swished, her expression became pained. The truth of the matter was, regardless of how she felt about Myst, she didn't want to lose Luke. This world was terrifying and crazy and home to way too many outrageous characters. Despite Jericho's kindness, Luco, Buck and the King's guards proved that not all humans were like David. And why not admit it – Shiva felt safer with Luke. He protected her, guided her… and she knew that she cared about him. His rescue in the prison, his words in the arena, his carrying Myst for miles during the run. How could she abandon him after that?

She sighed and pressed her head against his. "Okay, Luke," she said. "Let's see if we can work something out."

Luke's ears perked, and he wagged his tail hopefully, as Shiva dropped the link. Myst rubbed her neck with a grimace. The other wolves, relaxing around the shore of the lake, perked their ears and watched the two females with curiosity.

"I appreciate that," Myst said.

Shiva simply eyed Myst cautiously. "For starters, I refuse to believe that every human is irredeemable," Shiva said.

Myst massaged the nerve points where Drake had hit her in their fight. "Even Luco?" she asked.

Shiva grimaced. "Okay, Luco is definitely bad, but he doesn't represent everyone else."

"How are we supposed to know that?" Myst asked. "How are we supposed to know, when they can hide behind facades of kindness or nobility?"

Shiva's pack link glowed and she glanced at the link with speculation.

"This allows me to read thoughts and memories," she noted with a grin. "Should make it a little easier to figure out what any visitors want from us."

Myst scoffed. "What's there to figure out?" she asked. "All you'll see is what they want to take from us."

"That's your problem," Shiva replied. "You're so focused on the bad humans that you make it too easy for the few good humans to hate us and ignore your pertinent points."

"Humans like Luco hurt us when we didn't deserve it," Luke guessed.

"Exactly," Shiva said. "So why don't we focus on helping the demi-wolves. Or every wolf and canine in the world; what if we get them away from human territory? We form some kind of… sanctuary."

Myst rose up, stretching. "I don't disagree with that idea," she admitted.

Shiva lifted a claw. "But we only fight when they come after us. Only attack when they leave us no choice."

"That's a good plan, Myst," Luke noted.

"Yeah, I like it," several of the demi-wolves added, nodding to each other. Shiva's tail wagged at their support.

"Luco wants us to fight," Shiva pointed out. "That's why he hurt you; so you'd come after him, and he could create and force the dragons to fight his fight as well. So let's see what he does when he has to come after us, instead of us going after him."

Myst tilted her head. "You do realize that Luco won't come after us himself," she noted. "He'll use people. Like that 'Jericho' you were so hung up about."

Shiva simply flared the pack link in her claws with a grin.

"This allows me to read thoughts and memories," she reminded Myst. "If anyone's got ulterior motives, I'll find them." Her eyes narrowed. "And if Luco or any other humans do attack us, we will fight back. But it will be because we are defending the pack and they have done something to deserve it. NOT simply because they're human." A growl entered her voice. "Not like what you did to my father."

"Your what?!" Myst asked.

"I don't care what your reasons were," Shiva growled over her. "I don't care what species he was; David was my family. He was a good man and you killed him." She shook her head. "I won't forgive you for that." She glanced at the other wolves. "And if there's anyone here who has lost a master they loved to you as well… they don't have to forgive you either."

Myst frowned at the wolves. Darius and a few others looked away fearfully.

"What about the masters that abused them?" Myst demanded. "What about the ones that hated us for just being what we are? What about the ones who do *this?*"

She pointed at her scars; at the patterns that had been carved into her flesh. Shiva looked her full in her face, refusing to look away.

"Luco isn't the only one who's harmed us," Myst said coldly.

"Those scars on your face should remind us of where we don't want to go," Shiva responded, almost with compassion.

Luke took a knee beside her. He lifted a claw to one of the demi-wolves, who handed him Myst's mask.

"Don't forget to show Shiva what you showed me," he told Myst, pressing the mask into her claws. "Your love for our kind. Your commitment to our safety. When they come for us, looking to enslave or torment us, don't be the Killer of Man. Be the Hero of Wolves."

Shiva rested a claw on his shoulder, although her eyes didn't leave Myst's.

"Exactly," Shiva agreed. "don't just show me and the other demi-wolves the hero you claim to be; show the humans as well. Because when you become a monster to fight monsters…"

"You deserve what they deserve," Myst snarled sarcastically. "So, I've heard."

Shiva noticed the threatening tone, and raised her claw, her pack link flickering to life.

"Well, if lectures don't work," Shiva growled. "I'm more than willing to use force."

The previously quiet demi-wolves were on their paws, growling. Was Shiva going to challenge the Alpha? Sides were taken; it seemed like a fourth of the pack took to Shiva's side, while the remaining wolves clearly sided with their Alpha. Myst took the entire situation in.

"Stand down!" she commanded. Turning to Shiva, she said, "For the sake of peace among our pack, I agree to your terms." She held out a claw.

Shiva's tail wagged and Luke sighed in relief. Myst's loyalists grumbled but backed off. Their eyes shined when Myst gripped Shiva's claw, and she donned her mask.

"But soon enough," Myst promised. "You will see the truth as I have. Luco – and all the other humans like him - will never truly care about us the way you cared about them. The second they come to hurt us and take advantage of you, you'll need to be ready to follow up on everything you just said."

Shiva was silent at first. Though it still tore her heart to think about humans as cruel and merciless creatures, she couldn't deny what she had experienced.

She nodded, and shook Myst's claw again. "That's a Deal," she said.

The other demi-wolves crowded around Myst, as Shiva walked into the forest. She gazed up at the tall oaks – so similar to the trees she had roamed under as David's dog. She wasn't sure if it was the different location or just due to everything she went through, but the trees seemed smaller than before. Less imposing, but still magnificent.

The shuffle of paws broke her concentration, and she turned back to find Darius walking after her. She turned to him, tilting her head in curiosity.

"Um... hi," he mumbled.

"Hey," Shiva replied. "Darius, right?"

Darius's ears perked. "Y-Yeah. Wow, I... didn't know if you remembered my name or not."

Shiva chuckled. "One good thing about the Pack Link?" she replied, letting her tendrils form a screen that displayed Luke introducing Darius to Shiva. "Perfect memory."

He chuckled, before his expression became heavy. "Well, in either case," he said. "I wanted you to know... if anything happens between you and Myst... I had a good home too. A good master... and a lot of human friends. Myst may have meant well, but she took those things from me." He lowered his head. "I was too scared and nervous to confront her about it, but... if she doesn't remember what you said, I'm more than happy to help you remind her."

"Same here," another demi-wolf noted, walking up as well. Shiva's pack link recognized him as 'Marcus.'

"Me too," a third demi-wolf – Don - replied.

"And me," a fourth one – Sparks - said.

As more of the wolves that agreed with Shiva joined her, Shiva dared to hope that things could change. And yet… there was one particular wolf that wasn't among them. Until…

"Nothing's gonna happen between them," Luke's authoritative voice insisted.

The others turned to find Luke watching them. Shiva sighed, looking away.

"Luke, I'm not in the mood for another lecture," she said.

"Lectures?" Luke asked. "Can I fight those?"

Shiva smiled. "No."

"Can I eat them?"

"No."

Luke shrugged. "Well, then, I'm not in the mood for them either," he replied.

Shiva chuckled as he stood beside her, observing the forest. Luke hummed thoughtfully as he gazed up at the trees. Shiva nodded at Darius and the others, and they wisely backed off, leaving Luke and Shiva to their own devices.

"It's funny," Luke noted. "Before Myst found me, all I ever worried about was what I could eat and what I could fight."

"Do you… miss that life," Shiva asked.

"Yeah," Luke admitted. "It was simple. It made sense. I fought what I didn't like, and I ate what I did like."

Shiva's tail wagged. "Can I assume you didn't have many friends or pack mates?"

His voice was soft, but it carried a small element of sadness to it. "You can."

Shiva's smile softened. She touched his arm. "So, what changed your mind?"

"Nothing," he admitted. "If I'm honest, I want to keep things that way."

Shiva tilted her head. "Eating what you like?" She started to scooch away, even as her voice remained light-hearted. "Should I be concerned?"

Luke laughed. "No," he said quickly. "No, not like that, I promise."

Shiva relaxed, but still kept a watchful eye on Luke as he breathed in the scents of the forest.

"What I guess I'm saying is…" Luke tried again. "I like things simple. The dragons are cruel, and so are the humans. So, we fight them, to keep the ones that we like safe. Fighting fellow demi-wolves – many of whom I like…" He shook his head. "That doesn't sit right with me."

Shiva's tail drooped. She looked down with a nod. "Well," she said. "As long as Myst sticks to her word – shows herself more as a hero than a killer – then I'm willing to give her a chance."

"She will," Luke promised, giving a hopeful look to Shiva. "She has to. We don't have the cunning of humans or the strength of dragons. But we have each other." He offered his claw. "And that's all we need."

Shiva smiled softly and took his claw. Together they walked softly out of the forest and into the clearing by the lake, the rising sun's light sparkling on the water. They returned to their pack.

Though Shiva's heart still throbbed for David and Jericho, and other humans that held kindness in their hearts, she couldn't help but feel a sense of comfort as she re-joined the demi-wolf pack.

Luke and Darius and the other demi-wolves had pledged their loyalty to her. Even Myst managed to meet her with – at the very least - acceptance.

"And who knows," Shiva thought as she mixed back in with the pack, *"Maybe Myst can change. If I'm careful… maybe I can help her."*

When the howl of the demi-wolf hunting scouts sounded, bringing with them reports of prey, Myst led the pack into the forest. And Shiva ran with them, side by side with Luke and Darius, howling as they went.

Chapter 15: Let it be Peace

Shiva cautiously approached the forest clearing. The rising moon and the dusky light cast a purple and gold glow over the grass. Though the trees obscured what dwelled under them in shadow, Shiva detected the glint of metal. She could see the glitter of scales, and the flowing satin of a robe.

"This the place?" Luke asked, walking up beside Shiva. "Smells right, but…"

"Yeah," Shiva assured him. "It's the place." She glanced behind him. "Myst?"

The masked demi-wolf stepped out next to her. Myst surveyed the land before them with narrowed eyes.

"This is a mistake," she insisted. "You can't trust the word of a human."

"Some humans, maybe," Shiva admitted. She turned to Luke. "Do you trust me?"

Luke nodded. Myst hesitated, but she nodded all the same.

"Then don't trust the humans," Shiva replied. "Trust me."

The demi-wolves had no argument, and together, they followed Shiva out and into the clearing.

Shiva stopped, her nose twitching and her ears searching for sound. Luke and Myst tensed by her side. Although they couldn't see anything, the air was filled with subtle scents.

Then, out from the shadows, they appeared: The King, his black satin robes flowing in a non-existent wind. Flanking his left was General Drake, his face a mask of stone. On the King's right was Rocket, her eyes focused squarely on Myst just as Myst's were directly focused on her.

Unfortunately, Shiva could not focus on Rocket or Myst. She turned instead to the King. Though darkness concealed his face, his eyes still glittered from the shadows of his hooded crown. They locked with Shiva's brown orbs.

"Your Majesty," Shiva greeted.

"Hello again, Shiva," the King replied, chancing a glance at a glowering Myst. "Or should I say… 'Alpha' Shiva?"

Myst stepped forward, her low snarl causing Rocket to bristle and glow with flames.

"As you were, Rocket," the King said, blocking Rocket with his hand.

At the same time, Shiva blocked Myst with her claw, her eyes not leaving the King's. Myst's teeth bared at Shiva's intervention, but after a tense moment, the former Alpha stood down. The King inclined his head with a hum.

"I hoped the rumors were true," the King admitted. "That you did not share Myst's plans for conquest. But what is it that you want?"

"I don't suppose you want to just hand Myst over?" Drake interjected. "And let us forget what happened in the arena?"

Rocket stepped forward, but Shiva's pack link pulsed, causing the dragon to stop.

"I can't do that," Shiva replied.

Drake popped his knuckles. "If you won't hand her over," he said. "Then we must consider you an enemy."

"Let's not get ahead of ourselves, General," the King warned.

"Her pack considered you their enemy," Shiva refuted. "When they once called you friend." Shiva's pack link pulsed again, and memories floated between the two groups. *The time when dogs and humans stood side by side against the forces of nature.* "Before everything we cared about was perverted and destroyed by those who considered themselves Gods." Shiva gazed up at the King. "Humans like the man who tore our bond apart don't understand sentiments like friendship or forgiveness. Some canines don't either. They don't look for a fair word or a fair fight." She pointed at the king. "But I'm hoping you do."

The King tilted his head, as Shiva indicated Myst.

"I brought Myst because our resolve to fight against those that would oppress and kill us is not changed," Shiva explained. "But I am here because I believe there is another way." The image in her link changed, displaying a land where trees were hollowed out into dens. Where wolves hunted, played and prospered far from the lands of men. "Just as the wolf once lived alongside the bear and the antelope, so we shall again. We'll stay far away from humanity, only hunt what we need to live on. If no human shall trespass on the territory of the demi-wolves, so too shall no demi-wolf trespass on the territory of men."

For a long moment, there was silence between the groups. The King withdrew a flask from his robe, and took a long pull, his eyes not leaving Shiva's.

"You say you will leave us," he finally noted. "But... you said nothing about rejoining us...a fact that will break the hearts of humans such as Jericho." He smiled softly at the twitch of Shiva's tail. The hopeful grin that she barely suppressed. "Yes, she still lives. But she will be saddened by your choice to stay away from us."

"She will be saddened?" Drake asked. "My King, forgive me, but it's better that she be sad and alive, than happy and dead." He glared at Myst. "These creatures have caused more than enough pain and suffering for our kind."

Myst bristled. Shiva jerked her hand up, motioning for her to be silent. She hadn't missed the rising tension in the King's shoulders.

"And yet here this wolf stands," the King pointed out. "Asking for us to simply live in peace. No attempt at murder, no declaration of revenge... that I know of," he added with a wry grin.

Shiva glanced back at Myst and nodded. The masked demi-wolf growled, but stepped further back all the same. Shiva grinned hopefully up at the King, who shared her smile.

"It makes me curious…" The King's smile faded as he turned back to Drake. "Why did you not listen to your Rider and tell me about this 'Shiva' when you found her? Why did I have to find out about her when your dragon chased her across my city and terrified my subjects?"

"Connors…" Drake tried to say.

"No!" the King said sharply. "'Your Majesty.' Just as you are 'General.' A title I gave you because I hoped you would understand my desire to see our people reunited. But if the General of our greatest military force cannot recognize a chance for peace, then all we have done is suspect. Our subjects have to trust us, or we cannot help them."

"That trust goes both ways," Myst growled. "You either didn't know or didn't care about what your subjects did with our kind…"

"Whatever they did, murder was not the answer!" Drake insisted, turning his fiery glare on Shiva. "Something you could learn from."

Shiva's ears flattened, remembering Rider Buck. Her skin paled under her fur as the King gave her a curious look. The demi-wolf sighed.

"It's true." Shiva looked to Rocket. "What happened with Rider Buck was a tragedy. Not a day goes by where I don't wish that things could have turned out differently. I wasn't able to save him. But I can try to prevent anyone from dying like he did."

Rocket grimaced, looking away, but the King smiled.

"Then it seems to me," the King noted to Drake. "That the 'danger' you see is merely to your image that you and your dragons can do no wrong."

"They can't…" the General tried to claim.

"They can't?" the King demanded, turning fully to Drake. "Then explain why your dragon thought she could get away with attacking my town and committing wanton destruction?"

Drake paused, looking at Rocket. The dragon did not meet his eyes, guilt weighing her head.

"Not very heroic…" Myst muttered.

"Myst," Luke hushed.

"And while you're at it," the King continued over the wolves. "Explain your dragon's meaning of courage: striking when her victim had no hope of striking back. And keeping the excuse of 'they're evil' or 'dangerous' to deflect any blame." He turned to Rocket, who backed up as his eyes landed on her. "If Shiva was as great a threat as Myst, have the decency to face that wolf in proper combat, where the penalty for loss is a swift death. To drag it out over a long and brutal chase is sadism, not security."

"That's not fair!" Rocket insisted. "She killed my Rider!"

But even then, Rocket had doubt in her voice. And as Shiva stared at her, the dragon backed down, growling in self-loathing and conflict. The King, for his part, didn't even spare Shiva a passing glance.

"Did you not listen to a word she said?" the King growled. "Your Rider attacked her and she defended herself. If a human attacked you and relentlessly tormented you, could you honestly tell me you'd just let it happen?"

"A human isn't supposed to do that!" Rocket muttered.

Yet Shiva could see the doubt in her eyes. The memory of Luco's deeds cheapened the dragon's words in her mouth, unveiling the lie she once believed as truth.

The King's smile was somehow more frightening than his frown. "Ah. The source of the problem emerges."

Rocket tilted her head, as the King turned back to Drake.

"Tell me something else, my General," the King said. "When you made these fascinating creatures, you told them to protect the innocent, yes?"

"That's right," Drake replied. "Protect humanity."

Myst barked a laugh, but Shiva and Luke hissed at her for silence. Thankfully, the King didn't glance their way.

"A lovely answer, but not the answer to my question." The King sighed, turning back to Shiva. "It is a sad fact of man that, in the name of survival, we have become dependent on cunning, dishonor, and double-talk." He nodded at Myst and then turned to Shiva. "Let me prove that your faith in me is not misplaced." The King stepped forward. "In times long ago, men and dogs shared a bond that made us both better than we were apart." He offered his hand. "In the name of that friendship, let us co-exist again. If not as friends, at least in peace."

Shiva took his hand. "Then in peace," she agreed. After a pause, she spoke quietly, "I wish you well."

The King smiled softly, and released her claw. Then, the two groups parted.

As Shiva followed Myst and Luke, she couldn't help but glance back, as Drake and Rocket stared at their departing King in uncertainty.

"Your Majesty?" Drake asked.

"You may have created Rocket and her fellow dragons, General Drake," the King replied. "But you only made them with my express permission. Even then, you have clearly failed to teach them an incredibly vital lesson for doing their job." His eyes glinted as he turned to Rocket. "I will see you learn this lesson, Rocket, and I hope then, you will be able to truly put an end to the conflict that plagues our kingdom."

"Truly put an end?" The General demanded. "Con-…Your Majesty, I mean no disrespect, and I'm more than willing to see Rocket compensate you for any damages she has caused. But it's because of her and the other dragons that so many humans are still alive today. Shiva's different – I'll admit that. But Myst isn't. None of the other demi-wolves had a problem following her orders... orders that killed many humans."

The King was silent for a moment. He withdrew his flask and took another long pull. When he finally spoke, his voice was calm, but there was an authority in his tone.

"Though the wolves were a formidable threat, they are not humanity's worst enemy." He chuckled, and said, "From the sound of your voice, General, I believe you know this already. But you just don't want to believe it."

Rocket and Drake glanced at each other with alarm, Shiva's vision of Luco once again played before their eyes. The King moved to Rocket's side.

"But... wait a minute," Rocket said, as the King climbed onto her. "If humanity's worst enemy isn't Myst, then... who is?"

The King chuckled in sync with Luco's laughter from the vision, making Rocket dread the answer to her question, while Shiva couldn't help but yearn for it. Briefly, the King glanced at Drake, who was shaking his head. But the King ignored Drake's warning and turned back to Rocket.

"My brave dragon," he replied. "Humanity's worst enemy… is itself."

The General winced, as Rocket deflated. "But…" she whispered. "If humans aren't all good, who do I trust?"

"None of them," Myst said, as Luke pulled the dark demi-wolf after Shiva. Yet she kept her ears open as the King's final words drifted with the wind.

"That's the question of the century, isn't it Rocket?" the King continued. "While the General's actions are understandable, you must understand that innocents and humanity are not one and the same. If you cannot learn to make that distinction… then I shudder to think of what will become of the Roads of Gaia."

#

As the King spoke, he looked to the mountains, where the pale moon illuminated the gray, rocky heights. His eyes almost seemed to lock with Luco, who sat perched on the cliff side many miles away, watching.

In the light of the silver moon, Luco's scar deformed his face into a demonic smile. He chuckled, and left his perch, approaching the slumbering Blazy.

"Oh, don't you worry, 'your majesty,'" Luco declared. "Shiva may have foiled my first plan. But the great thing about life? You lose today, you win tomorrow." His smile widened as Blazy awoke. "I'll come up with something else. Just you wait."

Epilogue

In the comforting shade of the tree den, the newborn pups snuggled up against Shiva's white fur. Celine wriggled excitedly, her brown eyes open and her yellow fur sparking as she played with her pack link. Her brother Kodo grumbled in his sleep, his moonlight-white fur dim and his blue eyes hidden as he struggled to sleep despite his sister's rambunctiousness.

Shiva laughed softly at her daughter's antics. She supposed Jericho or David would be surprised at how quickly Celine and Kodo were conceived. But, demi-wolves don't really have the same hang-ups surrounding romance that humans do. Her species got right to the point of procreating, and the healthy pups were the promise of a better tomorrow. Luke had more than earned her trust and love over the years since the fight in the arena and the parlay with the King.

Granted, Kodo and Celine were too young to know the full splendor of the land in which they now lived. But the pack link made it easy for them. Even now, Shiva's tail wagged as she felt her daughter's mind rooting through the visions associated with their home. She was taking in the lush green forest and the large, ancient trees and rocky caves where the wolves carved out their dens. Along the hunting paths, prey abounded, and the bushes were bursting with berries. Fresh water tumbled down the rocky streams which reverberated with song in the deep woods.

Above all, Celine loved the minds of their pack mates. Those memories included old and new, including Darius's expansive memories of the farm on which he was raised or their father's tales of adventure and challenges. Shiva nearly got a headache trying to help her daughter process it all. Unlike Kodo, who seemed content to wait and let the material come to him, Celine ravenously hunted after every scrap of information she could find.

Too often, Shiva's heart raced as she struggled to hide darker memories from her daughter; in particular, experiences from wolves still loyal to Myst.

Almost as if she had been summoned, the masked demi-wolf appeared at the entrance of Luke and Shiva's den.

Only a hush from Luke could quell the burst of anger that rose up in Shiva at the sight of the white kitsune mask. Celine tilted her head, chirruping at the odd facade the former Alpha wore.

"It's okay, Celine," Shiva whispered, soothing her daughter with her tongue. "It's alright…"

She glanced at Luke, who turned to Myst with a wagging tail. "Welcome Myst," he lowered his head in respect. "The borders still safe?" he asked casually.

"Nothing to report for now," Myst replied, stepping closer to the pups. "What about them? How are they doing?"

"You could've checked through the link," Shiva replied coolly.

"Maybe," Myst agreed. "If you didn't block me every time I tried."

Luke sighed. "Shiva…" he moaned, as Shiva huddled around the twins protectively.

"You know how curious Celine is," Shiva insisted. "You know how many times I've caught her worming into Darius' memories?"

Luke's ears flattened as he thought. "Uh… five times?" he guessed.

"Twenty," Shiva replied.

"So, it's better that she stays out of my head," Myst conceded, easing closer. "We all agree on that? Good. Now let me have a look at those two."

Shiva's teeth involuntarily bared in protective instinct. But she suppressed her growl as Celine's foraging into the pack link faltered. The pup stepped towards Myst, her brown eyes locked on the demi-wolf's golden orbs, examining the former Alpha with curiosity just as much as Myst was examining her.

Cautiously, Myst extended a claw. But as the claw descended towards Celine, the tiny wolf pup's ears flattened. She let out a yip of uncertainty and retreated to her mother's waiting arms. Her cry woke her brother, who, surprised at this new arrival, gave a rougher yap at Myst, even jumping up and closing his jaws around one of her scarred forefingers.

Myst lifted him up, nodding in approval as he valiantly held onto her claw, tugging with equal parts ferocity and playfulness. She chuckled, even as Luke gently took Kodo back with a nervous grin. Carefully dislodging his son's teeth from Myst's claw, he passed the young pup back to Shiva, and tried to tend to his former Alpha. Myst seemed more intrigued by the pup, who was just as intent on soothing his twin sister as Shiva was on tending to them both.

"He is strong," Myst praised. "That's good. He will need to be ready for when the humans make their move."

Shiva sighed again, her gaze not leaving her children. "Myst," she said. "It's been almost two years. The King said we could trust him, and he's kept his word."

"Kings change," Myst replied. "So, do the minds of humans." She gazed back out at the land they had forged for themselves - the world in which Shiva hoped to introduce her pups to a better and more peaceful life. Myst shut her eyes and bowed her head. "I wish this could last forever, Shiva. Truly, I do." She turned her gaze back, and Shiva reflected on the memories in Myst's golden eyes – memories they both refused to expose to the pups. "But you can't trust humans. You can't trust them to let this last."

Shiva held her pups tighter, before Luke stepped gently between them.

"It will last," he said with steel in his voice. "If the humans try to change it…" He lifted his bared claws, and let the light of his mate's link flicker across it. "We will be ready."

Briefly, Shiva slipped into his mind. Thankfully, his mind was simple: *it merely showed him, Myst and the wolves standing at the border. Eyes set in determination, with the pack link shining between them like a barrier. Awaiting an unknown enemy that lay beyond the forest, in an unknown future.*

Yet, as Shiva tried to hide it, she noticed Kodo turning back to her. His moon-white fur glowing as his blue eyes gazed past her own and into her mind.

"What are we ready for?" his face asked, before Celine jumped on top of him.

"You better be ready for me, slow poke," her mind giggled with innocent glee. *"Now that you're awake, let's play."*

In trying to wriggle out of Celine's grip, Kodo only exacerbated his sister's exuberance. Shiva smiled as the two pups ran from her arms and play-fought around the den. Yet, as Myst and Luke walked away, talking quietly, Shiva couldn't help but look at Luke and Myst with concern.

"We will be ready," she tried to reassure herself. *"If Luco tries something... we will be ready."* She returned her gaze to her pups. *"For now, enjoy this time.*

There's no telling how long it will last, after all."

Made in United States
Troutdale, OR
10/29/2023